LUCY ROSE

Working

Myself to

Pieces & Bits

Also by Katy Kelly

Lucy Rose: Here's the Thing About Me

Lucy Rose: Big on Plans

Lucy Rose: Busy Like You Can't Believe

LUCY ROSE

Working Myself to Pieces & Bits

by Katy Kelly

ILLUSTRATED BY PETER FERGUSON

Delacorte Press

Big thanks to Molly Sternberg,
entrepreneur and Enchanted Beauty

Published by Delacorte Press
an imprint of Random House Children's Books
a division of Random House, Inc.
New York

This is a work of fiction. Names, characters, places, and incidents either are the product of the author's imagination or are used fictitiously. Any resemblance to actual persons, living or dead, events, or locales is entirely coincidental.

Text copyright © 2007 by Katy Kelly
Jacket illustration copyright © 2007 Peter Ferguson

Delacorte Press and colophon are registered trademarks of Random House, Inc.

www.randomhouse.com/kids

Educators and librarians, for a variety of teaching tools, visit us at
www.randomhouse.com/teachers

Library of Congress Cataloging-in-Publication Data
Kelly, Katy.
Lucy Rose : working myself to pieces and bits / Katy Kelly ; illustrated by
Peter Ferguson.—1st ed.
p. cm.
Summary: In her diary fourth grader Lucy Rose, lover of palindromes and big words,
records her adventures with friends Jonique and Melonhead, including their unorthodox
ways of raising money for the McBees to remodel their bakery.
ISBN 978-0-385-73408-0 (hardcover)—ISBN 978-0-385-90425-4 (Gibraltar lib. bdg.)
[1. Interpersonal relations—Fiction. 2. Family life—Fiction. 3. Diaries—Fiction.
4. Washington (D.C.)—Fiction.] I. Ferguson, Peter, ill. II. Title. III. Working myself
to pieces and bits.
PZ7.K29637Lwo 2007
[Fic]—dc22
2006028701

The text of this book is set in 14-point Goudy.

Printed in the United States of America

10 9 8 7 6 5 4 3 2 1

First Edition

For Steve Bottorff,
who will always be the man for me,
with infinite love

JANUARY

January 2

At 7:46 this morning my eyeballs were practically popping out of their lids from tiredness and all I wanted to do was laze about for 23 or more minutes under my pink dotty bedspread in my all-red room and practice my stretching in case it might make me get taller, which I need because there's a lot of shortness in my family, including me. Then I remembered about today and I got up so fast that if you saw me your head would spin.

I have never actually seen a spinning head but my grandmother, who's called Madam, says that whenever someone is speedy in the extreme, which I am just about all the time.

But my friend Adam Melon, who actually likes it when I call him Melonhead, which is lucky because that is all I ever do call him, says necks can't twist that far. I say probably some necks can under circumstances because Madam is not one who makes up stuff, plus she's the writer of a newspaper column that's absolutely full of directions for parents and is completely nonfiction.

So Melonhead and I have to have pretty many discussions about headspinning. The last time, he got the look of being exasperated with me, which is the same as being a little fed up, and he said, "Think about it, Lucy Rose. We're 9 years old. I used to live in Florida and you used to live in Michigan and we've been all over Washington, D.C., and Capitol Hill. We've even been to Maryland and Virginia but we've NEVER seen 1 single spinning head."

"I have on TV," I said.

"That's fake," he said. "Think about it."

I did think about it and what I thought was that he is right but I did not admit it because the thing about Melonhead is that, even though I feel a LITTLE fond of him, he's the sort who acts like he knows everything in this world, which is the exact kind of carrying-on that made me call him Melonhead in the first place. Also it's the reason that sometimes my ultra-best friend, Jonique, and I feel like we want to give him a sharp poke. Only we don't because when you are in 4th grade like we are, that behavior is called NOT APPROPRIATE.

If you do poke a person, even if it's a soft poke that hardly hurts, you get sent to Mr. Pitt's office that smells like old lunch and has posters about TEAMWORK and RESPECTING OTHERS. Then you have to listen to Mr. Pitt talk his head off until your ears go buzzy on the inside, and if you watch his beard go up and down, you could probably get hypnotized.

Plus those chats of his are so utterly dull that if the poking people were allowed to pick their consequences, which they certainly are not, they'd take getting squashed by Ashley, who is the snarkiest girl alive, over hearing 16 seconds more of Mr. Pitt talking about being a PEACEKEEPER who uses her SELF-CONTROL.

I know this from my personal experience.

That's what I was thinking about while I was brushing my teeth with my automatic toothbrush that came from my Glamma that lives in Ann Arbor and is shaped like a penguin. I mean the toothbrush, not my Glamma, who is only a little bit penguin-shaped, mostly around her stomach. At the same exact time I was thinking and brushing, I was also trying to make my head spin. My mom calls that multi-tasking, which is doing 2 or 3 things at once. Sometimes I do 5.

When my teeth were shined, I skied down the hall on my pink fuzz socks. That was to save my energy. Then I crash-landed in my mom's bedroom that looks utterly deluxe ever since she painted it the color of scrambled eggs, and I started singing at the tip-top of my lungs, "You gotta GET UP in the mornin'," until she finally did.

My mom rushed and brushed her teeth and I made the recommendation that she brush her hair at the same time for speediness. Then she hopped into her black yoga pants and purple sweatshirt. I was already wearing my orange shirt with blue fish on it and my green pants that have pink roses climbing up their legs. I wore my red cowgirl boots because I always do. Then my mom said, "Find the snowflake sweater Daddy gave you because . . ."

"Because 'Baby, it's cold outside,'" I sang,

which is an activity that I have to do every minute because I'm practicing for when I'm a star on Broadway.

"It's also a long walk to 7th Street," my mom said. "So stop writing and let's shake a leg."

"I am leg-shaking," I said. "But I'm bringing this new red velvet writing book with us because 1. I might think of a thing I have to write down and 2. Of all the books Pop ever gave me, this one is the absolute smoothiest and is a comfort to my hands."

Same exact day, only it's 9:16 AM in the morning

My mom and I dashed ourselves over to Constitution Avenue to pick up my grandparents, who were bundled and waving their arms off at us.

"Good morning, Lily," Pop called out to my mom.

"Hello, Old Sock," Madam said to me.

When she calls me Old Sock she means it in the complimenting way.

We walked fast, only whenever I saw giant snow

clumps we had to stop so I could climb up and get a view of the distance.

Melonhead was already at 7th Street, jumping around in front of the store that used to be Capitol Plumbing and stabbing the awning with a stick to jiggle the snow on top. Awning is the 2nd-newest word in my vocabulary collection that's called WOTD for Word Of The Day. It's the name of those puny tents that stick out in front of windows, which is a look I admire on stores but not so much on houses.

"Look out below!" Melonhead screamed, a split of a second before an avalanche hit Pop on his feet.

Then Melonhead yanked up his jacket sleeve and said, "I have been here for 7 minutes and 13 seconds."

"I bet you got a watch for Christmas," my mom guessed.

That comment made Melonhead give us a whole tour of it.

"I've never seen a watch with so many dials," Madam said.

My grandmother is a big believer in compliments. She says that even when something is not my cup of tea, which in this report means my style of watch, I should still come up with a pleasing thing to say because, according to her, most things have some good in them.

Pop says when you can't find the good thing, say SOME, like if you are having a chat with a hostess you can say, "That's SOME ham."

I went with Madam's advice since it's professional. "I have never in my life seen a watch with so many hands," I said.

"Or alarms," Melonhead said.

"Or glow-in-the-dark numbers," my mom said.

"Or clocks," Madam said, because under the 6 there's another clock that's as teensy as this O.

Pop said: "I believe it's the kind of watch FBI agents wear on top-secret stakeouts."

"I set the littlest clock on Peking time," Melonhead said.

"Excellent idea," Pop said. "I often wonder what time it is in Peking."

"Who doesn't?" Melonhead said.

"I don't wonder because Peking is in China and I am not."

Then Melonhead checked his Washington, D.C., clock and said, "Now I've been here for 8 minutes and 16 seconds and I still haven't seen the first McBee."

"This calls for patience," Madam said.

"This calls for cocoa," Pop said.

"Excellent-O," I said. "My teeth are chattering right out of my spinning head."

We zipped across the street, into Eastern Market, and I stamped my cowgirl boots until my toes stopped sparkling from cold. Melonhead went straight to the Market lunch counter.

"What would you headspinners like?" Pop asked.

"A cheeseburger with extra pickles," Melonhead said.

"It's breakfast time," I said.

"Right," he said. "I'll have onion rings too."

"And we'd like 3 donuts and 3 cocoas," Pop said.

The cook pointed his spatula at my mom and Madam and said, "What are the ladies having?"

"Just coffee," I said. "On account of their pants are too tight from Christmas."

"Thank you for explaining that," Madam said.

"You're welcome," I said.

We used up more minutes buying tangerines from Mrs. Calamaris and for something extra she gave Melonhead and me each a raw olive, which was fascinating to look at but not to taste.

"It's bitter," Melonhead said.

"Evil olive!" Pop said, pointing at it.

Hilariousness is a talent of his and I have it too. It's because we're both original thinkers. That is why when Pop said, "EVIL OLIVE!" I shouted, "PALINDROME!"

Palindromes are words that are the same in both directions, like my DAD, who's named BOB.

Now we are just sitting and waiting and Melonhead's making forehead marks on the front of the sausage displaying case and I'm writing down when he does it.

The Main Report of Today

The split of a second that I spotted the McBees' minivan, which, according to Melonhead, was at 10:24 AM Washington, D.C., time, we all raced back to the plumbing store. Only I was galloping and shouting "Yippee-yi-yo, cowgirl!" as loud as I possibly could, which Pop says is very loud indeed.

Jonique and I could not stop spinning around from excitement. My mom took photos of Mr. and Mrs. McBee and Aunt Frankie, who's Mrs. McBee's sister, smiling their lips off under the plumber's awning. Then Mr. McBee made a movie of Mrs. McBee holding up a key and saying, "Welcome to Baking Divas!"

"Future home of the best Red Velvet Cake on Capitol Hill," Mr. McBee said.

"The best in America!" I said.

"In the world!" Jonique said.

"When do you think that cake will be ready?" Melonhead asked.

He is an admirer of food.

Mrs. McBee opened the door and she and Aunt Frankie took a good look at the inside. Then Mrs. McBee said, "WHAT have WE done?"

We went inside to take our own looks. Right away Jonique's eyes went buggy. Then Mr. McBee turned off his camera. Pop, who is good at thinking up remarks, and Madam, who is one for finding bright sides, and my mom, who is great at comfort, were as quiet as rocks. I did not say it but I will tell you in private: I never saw a worse place.

For 1 thing, electricity cords were going every which way. For another, a lightbulb was hanging off the ceiling, which was spotty in a gross way and looking like it would be collapsing on us. When Aunt Frankie switched on that bulb, shadows from pipes made the big room in front look like the scariest forest in Transylvania or Albania or someplace where they have scary forests. Plus a person could choke to bits on the dust and I positively would have if I hadn't tied my yellow bandana over my nose. And the bathrooms were disgusting in the extreme and 1 had a puddle. The back room was full of spiderwebs. Also spiders.

"It looked better when we toured it with the real estate agent," Mrs. McBee said. "Plumbing supplies were on display."

"Did it smell better too?" Jonique asked.

Madam patted her on her head and said, "The building has been closed up. It's a little musty."

"I never smelled must before," I said.

I did not say what it smells like, which is P-U.

That was because of my thoughtfulness. I could tell the McBees were feeling like they were dejected to pieces. Dejected is a WOTD. It means when you are considerably down in the dumps.

All of a sudden, Adam came charging in from the spider room hollering his Melon head off. "Wow!" he shouted. "THIS is the greatest place on earth!"

January 3

Since Mr. and Mrs. McBee and Aunt Frankie have private discussing to do, and since we are still on winter vacation so there's no such thing as a school night, Madam sent Pop and me and Gumbo, the giant poodle, to fetch Jonique for a sleepover.

"How are you?" Pop asked the grown-up McBees.

"Overwhelmed," Mr. McBee said.

That is not a pleasing feeling. According to Pop, a person can be overwhelmed or underwhelmed. Overwhelmed is too much and underwhelmed is disappointed. I think the best thing to be is whelmed.

"Let's get going," Jonique said and waved her purple flowered suitcase at me.

Jonique is a fan of my grandparents and also of their extremely ancient house, which is on the gigantic side because of having 19 rooms that are mostly interesting including mine that I sleep in whenever my mom's working the overnight shift being an artist at Channel 6. I have never been inside of the attic because I am nervous of that room.

January 4

For breakfast I fixed my invention called Jamwiches that are made of raisin toast and 2 jams and 11 chocolate chips plus Marshmallow Fluff, which is the only food that Madam goes for that is made of empty calories. For fun, Jonique and I ate in the laundry room. Then we stood on top of the washing machine and taught Gumbo her dancing lesson by holding her Jamwich up in the air, which was minus the chocolate chips.

"She's doing such a great job of standing on her

own 2 legs that I believe she should be on the TV news," I said.

"Or she could have a show that other dogs could watch," Jonique said.

Jonique is the smartest cookie I know.

January 5

The McBees' house is usually a D-double-D-lightful place but lately they're having stress because the builder named Mr. Nathaniel had a delay because he should have started his job last week but didn't and, according to Mr. McBee, time is money. I don't actually get that because I have a lot of time and not so much money.

There's not 1 thing anybody can do about that delay because Mr. Nathaniel is IN DEMAND on account of he used to work for a company that made a Marriott from scratch.

Luckily enough, Mrs. McBee is having patience for waiting and loyalty for Mr. Nathaniel. "I was good friends with his late grandmother," she told us.

"Probally lateness runs in their family," I said.

It turns out that the grandmother's called late because she's dead.

"They should call that permanently late," I said. "So people can tell the difference."

January 6

My dad called and had a chat with my mom. I'm pretty sure it was about me because I'm their main topic.

Then my dad and I had our own talk about me and I told him, "Today was back-to-school."

"I go back tomorrow," he said.

"Even though it was the freezingest walk ever, I was stuffed with happiness to be back in Room 7," I said. "We got to go in early because of it being 32 degrees or under and Mrs. Timony was visiting Mrs. Mathur's room so there was extra added wildness."

"Really?" my dad said. That was a joke because when you're a junior high teacher you know wildness.

"Hannah was telling about going to England to see her mum's mum, which is English for her grandmother," I said. "Kathleen was showing her shoes that her Grandma Mary got from the outlet mall in New Jersey and Sam was balancing on Mrs. Timony's rolling chair and telling Amir, 'I got a chemistry set for Hanukkah and Melonhead and I are going to make potions and they might be the exploding kind.'

"Amir said, 'Fantastic,' to that," I said. "Last year he didn't know English. This year he knows exploding and potion. I told him: 'Amir, next year you will most likely be a genius.' "

"It sounds like it," my dad said.

"You can't guess what happened next," I said.

"Try me," he said and I did.

"Marisol, who's usually the quietest, told everybody, 'My Tía Angelina rode on a Greyhound all the way from Uvalde, Texas, to Washington, D.C.,' and Melonhead shouted out, 'I LOVE those dogs!' But Marisol said, 'This Greyhound was a bus. It had a built-in bathroom and movies on the ceiling.' Then Melonhead said, 'It would be a lot better if your aunt came by dog.' "

"Probably not for the dog," my dad said.

Then he asked me, "How was Ashley?"

She's that absolute pest of a girl.

"Actually, she was nice enough to ask me, 'What did you get for Christmas, Lucy Rose?' " I said.

"Her manners are improving," my dad said. "What did you say?"

"Nothing because the bell rang and Mrs. Timony came in and said, 'Let's start the new year off on the right foot,' which made Melonhead yell, 'I'm left-footed!' and go wild with his hooting," I said.

"Of course he did," my dad said.

"His hoots caused Bart Bigelow to make rude noises, which is a thing he loves to do anytime," I said. "Mrs. Timony had to give them pointy looks."

January 7

Ashley got behind me and Jonique at morning line-up and said, "You didn't tell me what you got."

She said it in a friendly voice that made me think she might have a new year's resolution about her attitude, so I did the encouraging thing and made a smile. And, since Madam says it's not thoughtful to talk about belongings in front of people, I said, "Gifts."

"Like what?" Ashley asked.

"Good stuff," I said.

"If it's so good why don't you say what it is?" Ashley said, and her voice had some snark in it.

I made my shoulders go shruggy.

"Because your gifts were stupid," Ashley said.

That made me bursting mad and my hands automatically went on my hips and I said, "For your information, I got ice skates and markers and 4 books and the original Broadway cast recording from *Hairspray*. Plus I got professional hair gel that's kiwi smelling and a pink and orange bulletin board that Madam and my mom made themselves with red ribbons on it and my dad wrote me a poem and gave me a sweater and these pink jeans that I'm wearing and this new yellow bandana because my old one got faded. PLUS my Aunt Pansy gave me paints and I got a cooking lesson from my Uncle Mike and Aunt Max and now I know how to make a whole, complete dinner out of chicken and artichokes, which I

am sure you DO NOT. Also I got stick-on earrings and a genuine parasol that was made in the country of Japan out of paper and sticks."

"I TOLD you she got hardly anything," Ashley said so loud that the whole class could hear.

Marisol's voice came out whispering. "It's a LOT to me," she said.

"Trust me, it's NOT," Ashley said and she made her eyeballs roll around in their sockets like they were loose. "It's dumb junk that NObody would like. Who thinks cooking artichokes is a present? Who wants a bulletin board that's not from a store? Stick-on earrings are for LOSERS."

The ultra-sickening part was that Jonique heard that insult and she was the giver of the stick-ons, which I say shows her caring, because I've been utterly desperate to get pierced ears ever since I was 8 and I'm not allowed until I'm in the double digits, at least.

Then Ashley started bragging her blond head off. "I got REAL earrings made of REAL GOLD and OPALS which, by the way, are PRECIOUS GEMS. I also got a Spin Art machine and 7 movies and a CAMERA and a GIFT CARD and these BOOTS that are REAL SUEDE and a charm bracelet and a purse and an ELECTRIC GUITAR and 6 OUTFITS and a skateboard and a TV FOR MY ROOM."

I could not believe about the TV.

I looked to see if Marisol could believe but I think her mind was feeling stunned because her mouth was stuck open and her eyes looked like they were dejected. That was the exact second I figured out that Madam's rule is a good one because I could tell that all the showing off made Marisol feel puny and that made me feel puny for doing it.

"Wow," I said so Ashley would be quiet.

Ashley made a smirk at me. Then she looked at everybody looking at her and said, "My dad took me to Hawaii and I saw palm trees and surfers and hotels and everything."

That's when Mrs. Timony came up and said, "Aloha, Ashley! Aloha, class! Let's find our indoor voices and go inside."

When Melonhead looked inside Mr. Nathaniel's van that's jammed to its brims with tools, he had to do his King Tut strut all over the sidewalk, even though anybody could tell Mr. Nathaniel is not the strutting type.

Also, he's not the cheerful type because after he frowned all over the store, he looked at Mrs. McBee and said, "No, you didn't."

He meant buy it.

"Yes, they certainly did," Jonique said.

Mr. Nathaniel climbed up the ladder and jammed his fingers at a ceiling square and said, "You got a leak."

"Can I see it?" Melonhead asked him.

"Boy, you better get off that ladder," Mr. Nathaniel told him.

Then he knocked on the ugly wood walls and made a scrape on the plaster wall with a screwdriver, which made dust puffs get on me because I was standing next to him in case he needed an assistant, which he didn't because Melonhead was hogging that job.

After he finished checking, Mr. Nathaniel told Mrs. McBee, "Let me fool around with some numbers."

I have no earthly idea how number fooling is supposed to help.

January 10

Jonique and I opened the store door and I had to holler, "Yippee-yi-yo, cowgirl! The must is gone!"

"You can tell the difference?" Mrs. McBee asked.

"Can I ever!" I said. "Pine-Sol is one of my Numero Uno best smells."

"Wait until cakes are cooking," Jonique said and she made a smile like she was feeling dreamy.

"I'm glad you have faith in us," Aunt Frankie said.

"Everybody does," I said.

"Amen to that," Mr. McBee said.

He did not smell 1 speck like Pine-Sol, but I

didn't say that because Madam says a person's smell is a topic that never gets mentioned by polite people, which I am a lot of the time and she is all the time.

Mr. McBee wiped his head sweat on his shirt and said, "I hauled the old pipes to the dump, Lola. But I left the copper pipes in the cellar, in case the plumber can put them to use."

Lola is the same as Mrs. McBee.

"I married a good man," she said and hugged his middle.

"Hardworking, too," Aunt Frankie said.

"This was an easy day," Mr. McBee said. "Tomorrow I'm going downtown to apply for building permits."

That's when the city permits you to do things and according to Mr. Nathaniel, that chore could make a person feel exasperated to death.

January 11

Everybody would love to be Jonique and me today on account of our friend that's named Mrs. Zuckerman asked us, "Why don't you girls call your mothers and see if it's okay to stay for supper?"

"At the Retirement Home?" Jonique asked.

"We are dazzled to bits by that invitation," I said.

"Really?" Mrs. Zuckerman said.

"It's been one of our dreams to eat here," I said. "That dining room looks like it's a divine restaurant."

"And they have butter squares that are wrapped in golden foil," Jonique said.

When we sat down, Mrs. Zuckerman told the server, "The girls and I will have Chicken à la King."

Then she told us, "The meat loaf disagrees with me."

"I disagree with YOU," Mrs. Hennessy said.

Mrs. Zuckerman didn't say anything, which I say shows her maturity because even though we are wild for Mrs. Hennessy, I believe Mrs. Zuckerman is not.

Mr. Woods, who has manners galore, gave Mrs. Hennessy his lemon Jell-O square with peach specks stuck to the inside.

"Thank you, my spicy friend," Mrs. Hennessy said.

"It's my pleasure, Flora," Mr. Woods said.

Mrs. Hennessy used to have a better way with her words.

P.S. I wish I was a King because I am crazy about Chicken à la.

January 12

While we were at school, Mr. Nathaniel was at the plumbing store patching up the roof leak because, even though the snow melted, he says we're bound to get more weather.

That remark is not at all sensible but I didn't say so because I did not want to make him feel testy with me.

On the inside, the Divas went wild pulling up the floor that's made of brown linoleum with reddish streaks and not the interesting kind of streaks, either. I know because Mrs. McBee told Madam, "That pattern is Hideous."

I would never buy a pattern named Hideous but probably the plumbers got it for a bargain.

The floor under Hideous is definitely not. It's made of black and white tiles that have 6 sides and are as big as a nickel and connected in a pattern that's mostly white with some black daisy shapes. Around the edges are puny square tiles that look like they're braided but aren't. They're mosaic.

"This floor is famous!" I said. "They have one like it at the Smithsonian museum."

Mrs. McBee said, "I don't think it's valuable but I do think it's beautiful."

It wasn't at first because the plumbers used globs of black glue to stick on the Hideous and the Divas had to scrub it off with chemicals.

Now Mrs. McBee's nails are ruined forever.

January 13

On our afternoon walk to the S.E. Neighborhood Library I told my mom, "In 3 ways Ashley is lucky."

"Name them," my mom said.

"1. TV in her room. 2. Pierced ears. 3. Her dad lives in Maryland so she can visit anytime," I said.

"I wish Ann Arbor were just a Metro ride away," my mom said.

"I wish it too," I said. "I miss Daddy."

"Of course you do," my mom said.

Then I changed to a new subject because my mom is the kind who utterly loves to consider people's inside feelings.

January 14

I called my dad the minute I got home and I told him, "At recess Ashley came right up to me and shrieked her head off, 'A poem is NOT a present, you know.'"

"Well, I'll show her," my dad said.

"What are you going to do?" I asked him.

"Write more poetry, of course," he said.

About 32 or more minutes later I got this from e-mail:

"From her nose to her toes, I love
    Lucy Rose.
From her bandana to her banana
From her cute suits to her red boots
My love is true and not a fad
That's because I'M HER DAD."

Under that it said GTG for Got To Go, which is a palindrome and also the truth because he has to have a parent-teacher talk about a kid named Otis who is not one for behaving. This very morning Otis put 30 catsup packs under the toilet seat in the boys' bathroom and when a boy named Zach sat on it catsup exploded everywhere and Zach's pant legs looked like they were bleeding and so did the bathroom floor.

I got out a postcard that was painted by me and has a picture of the Capitol dome that I can see through my window without getting out of my bed. On the back I wrote:

You're the best dad
I ever had.
You teach at Junior High.
You love berry pie.
You wear glasses
And give out hall passes.
Luckily your head's not made of wood.
You love me and that is good.
You eat Cheetos and drink water
I love you because I'M YOUR DAUGHTER.

January 15

One thing I can tell just by looking is that the Divas' nerves are utterly raggedy. Plus I heard Mrs. McBee tell Madam, "I'm in a state of panic."

That is not like a United State. It is an expression. Here's the other thing: Even Sam Alswang's infant of a sister would say Aunt Frankie's got anxiety if she could talk. I mean Julia the baby, not Aunt Frankie, who, according to Mr. McBee, can talk until her tongue goes numb.

January 16

Jonique and I did the Olympics for my mom, who loved it so much she said: "I have never seen gymnastics performed in such an original way."

Madam's praise was, "I can't get over how you made such official-looking costumes out of bathing suits, fuchsia curtain fringe, and tinfoil."

"Plus glue," I said. "Glue is the secret ingredient."

Jonique and I were about to do a repeat show but

my mom got 1 of her brilliantine ideas and said, "Maybe Ms. Bazoo needs Bingo callers."

By the way, I am the person who invented brilliantine. It means the same as brilliant, only better.

Jonique and I jumped into action and our clothes. I put on my pink petticoat skirt that's shorter than it used to be on account of I grew a puny bit and it shrunk a lot and also my lime green knitted tights that make my legs feel like they're sweating. For extra, added style, I got my red sparkle sweater and my mom's necklace that's made of orange balls and I tied my bandana in a bow so it would be a compliment for my red hair. Now we are off to whelm the retired.

January 16, only now it's 4:37 PM

Ms. Bazoo felt like she was thrilled out of her mind to see us. Since it wasn't a Bingo day she made the surprising announcement of: "Lucy Rose Reilly and Jonique McBee are here to perform an impromptu concert."

Then she rushed to the social hall and Jonique

and I had to race our legs off to keep up with that speeding lady and everybody was flocking behind us because we have fans galore at the Home.

Usually being on a stage makes me feel like I'm rolling in happiness but today my nerves were in a jangle of embarrassment plus the state of panic. That was due to us being in a dreaded circumstance and me not having 1 shred of a plan to save us. All the retired were sitting, except for Dr. Chu, who was gliding around with her walking stand that has tennis balls on its legs, and Mr. Woods, who was rolling Mrs. Beaufont's wheelchair to the front so she could have a view.

At the last split of a second I got the sharp idea to act like a ventriloquist, only quieter. So, while I was making my curtsey I leaned my head into Ms. Bazoo's side and I whispered at her, "Saaaave us, Ms. Bazooooo! We DON'T KNOW any impromptu songs."

"Are they country music?" Jonique said a little softly.

Probably we were too quiet because Ms. Bazoo just picked up the microphone and talked to the audience. "Welcome, everyone! We're in for a treat today!" she said. "Now Lucy Rose and Jonique will begin their impromptu concert."

That made my stomach feel spinny.

But Ms. Bazoo kept on talking: "By IM-PROMPTU," she told the audience, "I mean the girls have NOT PLANNED AHEAD so they will sing whatever they decide at the moment."

That comment gave me fast relief. "I'm impromptu just about all the time," I told the microphone.

"Now for 'Somewhere Over the Rainbow,'" Jonique said and we took off singing.

Near the end we made a dedication to Mrs. Hennessy because she's our favorite. We didn't announce that part because of not wanting to cause jealousy but we did sing her best song, which is, "Tonight You're Gonna Sleep in the Bathtub." It's about a man named Mr. Jones who comes home too late and Mrs. Jones gets unhappy with him.

We learned it from Pop.

For my grandest finale I sang the solo of "Hello,

Dolly," and when I was being Dolly, I made myself sashay. That place went wild.

January 17

Jonique and Hannah and Melonhead came to dinner at Madam & Pop's and afterward we got to cook marshmallows in the fireplace, which was good because dinner was not. It was squash casserole that, according to Madam, is loaded with vitamin A, which turns out to be a pretty bad-tasting vitamin.

P.S. Melonhead kept catching his marshmallow on fire on purpose.

January 18

I was thumbtacking up my book report about a family that makes all their money by catching clams and I heard Ashley tell Marisol, "Lucy Rose is D-U-M. That book is so 3rd grade."

That made me double steaming because 1. It is

not and 2. I am not. So to show my smartness I said, "I did my report impromptu."

"What does that mean?" Ashley snarked at me.

"It means without planning," I said. "Just dashing it off at the very moment."

"I can tell that by looking at it," Ashley said.

That was an irritation to me because even though I meant to say impromptu, I did not mean to say my report was dashed and unplanned.

The electricians, who have the names of Hank and Chester and are cousins, are spending 6 days at the Divas' store putting in wires that are not a fire hazard, which I say are the best kind to get.

Since Hank is 1 year older, he's the boss of Chester but Mr. Nathaniel is the boss of Hank and the City Inspector is the boss of everybody.

P.S. My dad keeps my poem on his desk at school. I told him, "I taped your new one to the bottom of my desk top, where Ashley can't see it but I can read it every time I open my desk, which is over 11 times an hour."

January 20

After morning greetings, Mrs. Timony gave us the news that every week or so we're having oral reports on different United States and she said, "I want your presentations to be relaxed and I'm especially interested in hearing about states you've visited."

Then she called on Hannah to make an example, and Hannah told about double-decker buses in London, even though England is a country not a state. I say that's okay on account of she's a little new to America and hasn't been to so many states.

"Do those double-deckers have movies and bathrooms?" I asked.

"No," Hannah said. "Just upstairs and downstairs."

"That's still good," I said.

Robinson asked her, "Did you ever see a castle or a king or queen?"

"Anybody can see Buckingham Palace just by

walking by it," Hannah said. "But royals don't just sit around in the yard waving at people."

"I saw Queen Elizabeth," Amir said and everyone gave him a stare. "Only she was on a stamp," he said and made a laugh.

"The Queen Elizabeth that's a cruise ship uses 1 gallon of fuel to move 6 inches," Melonhead said. Lately he's gone crazy over facts. I have no idea where he gets them.

"Last question for Hannah," Mrs. Timony said.

Ashley jumped up and said, "I think Hannah did a good job, considering her talk was impromptu."

"Excellent word choice, Ashley!" Mrs. Timony said.

"It means she didn't plan it ahead," Ashley said and smiled like she was famous.

"That's a good definition," Mrs. Timony said, and made a beaming look at her. "Now, I want each of you to decide which state you'd like discuss. We'll start tomorrow with Ashley, who recently went to Hawaii."

On the walk home I told Jonique, "That Ashley is nothing but a word thief."

"Who should be ashamed," Jonique said.

"A word thief who should be very ashamed but isn't and gets to go 1st and I bet her talk will be full of hula dancers and brags," I said.

"No doubt," Jonique said.

"I am so mad I could spit," I said.

But I didn't because, according to Madam, ladies don't.

January 21

On our way to buy the daisies that my mom thinks will scare away winter, Pop said, "Let's hear the Scoop du Jour."

That means Scoop of the Day.

"The Scoop du Yesterday was Ashley's terrible behavior," I said. "I was too steaming to talk about it."

I told the whole irritating story and I said, "Now Mrs. Timony thinks Ashley's the smartest and she gave her the reward of doing her state talk today."

"How did that go?" Madam asked.

"It didn't because she was absent," I said.

Madam made a sorrowful face. "Old Sock, try to

remember Ashley does things like this because she's not sure of herself," she said.

"Madam," I said. "You do not know Ashley."

Madam smiled and said, "Well, maybe time and sympathy will turn her around."

"There's only 1 thing that will turn Ashley around," Pop said.

"What's that?" my mom asked.

"A merry-go-round," Pop said.

That made us crack up like we were hyenas. Not the tame kind, either.

January 22

For his Florida report Melonhead gave out pictures of Mr. Melon's Congressman boss that are signed by him personally and it's my 1st autograph made by a famous person.

During comments afterward Ashley said, "I do not think Congressmen are interesting."

That remark was maddening to me so I said, "I would say Melonhead, I mean Adam, did a great job because I never knew that flamingos are pink because they eat shrimp and if they didn't their feathers would be nothing but white, which would be utterly dull."

"Thank you, Lucy Rose," Mrs. Timony said. "I like the way you focused on the positive."

"You're extremely welcome," I said.

January 23

Since Mr. McBee was working on his accounting and Mrs. McBee and Aunt Frankie had suffering arms, the Divas came to our house to eat stuffed shells and red sauce that my mom bought at Vace on the way home from work.

"Are you sure you still want us?" Mrs. McBee asked my mom. "We're a mess!"

My mom laughed, which I think was rude.

"Of course we do!" I said. "You come right in and relax yourselves."

"You have to hear our news," Aunt Frankie said.

"We uncovered a treasure," Mrs. McBee told us.

Aunt Frankie said, "Lola was on the ladder,

taking down those awful suspended ceiling tiles, and would you believe there's a tin ceiling underneath?"

"I would believe it," I said.

"Me too," Jonique said.

"What's suspended?" I asked.

Now suspended is my WOTD. It means when something is just hanging there.

"We spent the whole day unscrewing the metal strips that hold the tiles in place," Mrs. McBee said.

"What's the ceiling like?" my mom wanted to know because tin ceilings come in designs.

"It has a wreath pattern," Mrs. McBee said. "But right now it's painted silver and caked with dirt."

"I thought you were going to say the treasure you found was opals," I said.

"I wish," Aunt Frankie said. "We could use them to pay for the new furnace or the old wiring."

Then Mrs. McBee gave her a sharp-eye look and Aunt Frankie stopped her sentence very short and my mom blurted, "Girls, it's time for you to go to the kitchen and butter the bread."

The whole time we were buttering, those ladies

sat in the living room and ate Cotswold cheese and talked so softly that they were the only ones who could hear themselves.

January 24

I woke up so early there was darkness outside and I started thinking about my dad. What I thought was, "What if he is oversleeping?" I decided I'd better save his neck from that.

We had a shortie chat on account of he was extremely sound asleep. "See?" I said. "A wake-up call could be a good favor."

But it turned out his sleeping was on purpose.

Sometimes I forget when it's Sunday.

January 25

Now I know the topic of that talk the Divas had with my mom.

"Mr. Nathaniel says the bakery needs more work and more money than he thought," Jonique said.

"How much more?" I asked.

"Tons," she said.

"Does that count buying spoons and butter and those waxy paper squares that bakers need so they don't get fingerprints on the donuts?" I asked.

"I don't know," Jonique said. "My dad's trying to figure out how to make things cheaper."

For the whole time that Pierra Kempner was reporting on Wisconsin, the cheese state, Ashley did nothing but draw palm trees on her notebook, which I call showing off and Jonique agrees.

The Inspector gave Hank and Chester a sticker for doing a great job on the electricity. It says Passed and it's taped on the front window so everybody that goes by can see it and say, "Congratulations!"

I called my dad and said, "Yippee-yi-yo, cowgirl! I'm the writer of Paper of the Week!"

"What's it about?" my dad wanted to know.

"My friend Mrs. Hennessy," I said.

Then he sang "You are the Champion of the World" to me.

"That song gives me esteem," I said.

"That's why I sing it," he said.

Pop and Madam and my mom and Gumbo took me for a nighttime celebration walk around the Supreme Court and I told them that my paper is hanging on the bulletin board by the principal's office, which is the absolute best place a paper can be. Then we stopped off at Roland's Market and I got a Tootsie Roll for a present and Pop told the cash register lady, "If you're looking for something great to read, you might want to drop by my granddaughter's school and check out the main bulletin board."

She said she'd keep that in her mind.

That made me feel so delightful that I was

beaming in my face for the whole rest of the walk and without even knowing what I was thinking I blurted out, "I'm actually a smidge sorry that Ashley couldn't do her Hawaii report."

"Why couldn't she?" my mom asked.

"On account of having stage fright," I said. "Which is odd to me since she is one who loves to be the star."

"Yes, she is," Pop said.

"I am another one," I said.

January 29

Now that the Divas' tin ceiling is painted white, Pop calls it "A thing of beauty and a joy to behold."

"That's true," I said. "If I was the one to pick, I would have painted it red and gold."

"I'll bet the ladies never thought of that," Pop said.

January 30

When Jonique answered the phone I yelled, "I am having the brain storm of the century," so loud that

47

if a frail-feeling person heard, their legs would most likely start collapsing on the spot.

Jonique rode her scooter through a storm of wild rain and I was waiting right by the door with my White Owl box that Eddie at Grubb's drugstore gave me because otherwise it was going to be trash.

After I showed her my Michigan nickel that's collectable and my golden ring from Glamma, I said, "This is the money I was saving in case I ever need to buy a tuba, which I was thinking might be better to play than the cello I already do play."

"You've got $9?" Jonique asked me.

"Yes," I said. "Every Christmas Madam gives me $1 for every year old I am. This year, I'm giving it to the Divas to pay for the bakery."

"Too bad you're not 67," Jonique said.

"That's for sure," I said.

"What about your tuba?" Jonique asked me.

"That was just a fad I was having," I said.

We zippered the dollars in her raincoat pocket for safety and scooted ourselves to the McBees'. When we got there my feet were absolutely drowning inside my cowgirl boots.

Jonique's bank, which looks like a piñata only smaller because it would take too much money to fill a real one, had $8.72 in it that Jonique was saving up to buy the sparkling purple 2-wheeler she goes moony over in the window at Capitol Hill Bikes. The bike, I mean. Jonique is not one for making a display of herself in store windows.

"Let's go give it to the Divas," Jonique said.

But I said: "Let's wait and do jobs for pay so we can surprise them with a huge pile of money."

Then we practiced bouncing until Aunt Frankie said cut it out before we crashed through the ceiling.

FEBRUARY

February 1

I was sliding around on my stomach under my bed doing a search for my spotted sock and I got ANOTHER smartie idea.

I told my mom while we were cooking French toast and here's what she said: "Count me in!"

After we ate I called Pop and Madam and I said: "My original thinking is going to save the day."

"I knew it would," Pop said. "How?"

I gave them their jobs.

"We're delighted to be a part of your plan," Madam said.

At school I told Mrs. Timony, "Let's get to work because I am feeling brilliant like you can't believe."

After I wrote my homework paragraph about my delightful life, Madam and Pop and my mom and I ate Senate Navy Bean Soup, which is what they feed Senators every single day and if I ever got elected, the 1st thing I'd do is vote for a new food. But tonight, I was in such a rush to get to the McBees' that I drank that soup in 13 of my quietest slurps. Madam feels very appalled by the loud kind.

Since I was the one that thought up the idea, I got to be the one to say, "Divas, I have an announcement."

"Let's hear it," Mrs. McBee said.

"It's actually a plan and it has lots of parts and lots of people and one is my mom because she can be the artist who paints Baking Divas on your awning. For free, because this plan is a money-saving one," I said.

Mrs. McBee started to talk but my mom interrupted, which I have to say is against the rule in our family but she made an exception and said, "Please, let me do this, Lola."

Pop said, "I'm the master of caulk and spackle."

"Jonique and I can do everything," I said.

"Except sawing," Jonique said.

"And electric drilling," I said. "Madam isn't much of a driller either but she is the best at bargains."

"I love an auction," Madam said. "I'll go with you. We'll buy a lot of equipment for a little money."

"What's an auction?" Jonique asked Madam.

"They're the same as sales," I said. "Only it's like a contest because instead of having prices, people hold up number signs and the last one waving is the winner because they will pay the most. It's hard to keep up with because the person in charge that's called Auctioneer talks the whole time and it sounds like, 'Eye-gut-1-do-eye-ear-2-4-7-soul.' "

"You're good at auctions?" Jonique asked Madam.

"Very," Madam said. "Because I learned from my mistakes."

"Once she was trying to get 1 chandelier and she

accidentally bought 6," I said. "The best one is made of nothing but pink crystals that swoop."

Mrs. McBee stood up. "I'm lucky to have such dear, kind, loyal friends and you're right, this project is so much harder than we imagined," she said. "But we can't let you do our work."

"Yes you can," I said. "When a person has a dream their friends should help."

"I think that's right, Lola," Mr. McBee said.

"I know that's right," Aunt Frankie said.

Mrs. McBee let out her breath for the longest time and then she said, "Thank you."

"Now you have all the helpers you need plus 2 Junior Divas," I said.

"We've always had 2 Junior Divas," Mrs. McBee said.

For some reason that made the grown-ups laugh like they were nuts.

February 3

I told my Save the Day Plans to Melonhead on our walk to school. Here's what he did: Turned around and ran top-speed to my grandparents' and pulled on their absolutely ancient doorbell until Pop answered.

"You said I'm the man to have in a tight spot," Melonhead said in a shaking mad voice.

"You are that man," Pop said.

"You said I'm brilliant at figuring out new ways to use old toilet parts," Melonhead said.

"It's a rare and wonderful talent," Pop said.

"And you said that if you ever needed to clean your chimney by dangling a small boy upside down from the roof that I'm the small boy you would pick to dangle."

"Absolutely," Pop said.

"Then how come I'm not your assistant for fixing the Divas' bakery?" Melonhead asked him.

"You are my assistant," Pop said. "That's automatic. I wouldn't take the job, otherwise."

"Oh," Melonhead said. "That's good because I have always wanted to spackle."

"You will," Pop said.

Then Pop drove us to school so we wouldn't be late. He was still wearing his pajamas.

February 4

On the walk home from school Melonhead said, "Did you think up a moneymaking scheme yet?

"No," I said. "It's hard to manage 2 Save the Day Plans at one time, plus school and cello playing. Do you have ideas?"

"You could go on a game show," he said.

"I think the shows that give money for prizes only let grown-ups on," I said. "Which isn't fair since they're the ones with the jobs and kids are not."

"We can start a business, like the Divas," Jonique said.

"Brilliantine, my queen!" I said. "Only ours won't be the kind that makes you have to buy a plumbing store."

"We can sell hot chocolate," Jonique said.

That's what we're doing on Saturday and it's a good thing too because that air-conditioning Mr. Nathaniel ordered is completely expensive.

Pop was typing away in his office when we got to his and Madam's house. Instead of saying, "Hi," he said: "I've got to interview a man about an emu."

"E-moo?" Jonique asked.

"It's a big, rather unattractive bird," Pop said. "This man has a farm full."

Why I do not know.

"Ask him if emus have puny brains," I said.

"Okay," Pop said. "I will."

"Good," I told him. "Because according to Melonhead, an ostrich's eyeball is actually bigger than its brain. And emus could be that same situation."

"That's news I can use," Pop said and he got right to work asking questions because his magazine editors want that emu story pronto by Monday. Jonique and I went off to make a search of the kitchen cabinets.

"Don't tell that I walked on the counter in my socks," Jonique said.

Mrs. McBee is big on acting sanitary and having

hygiene, which means ultra-clean and completely against germs, only hygiene is for people and sanitary is for things. I hope 1 day I meet somebody named Jean so I can say, "Hi, Jean," every time I see her.

"Here's quinoa grains that Madam says are just the thing for Pop's health and Pop says are just the thing for making paste," I said.

"What are kippers?" Jonique asked.

"Fish that are brown and taste exactly like salt," I said.

"P-U," she said and put that can back.

"Very P-U," I said. "But Pop fancies those fish."

Hannah says that in England fancy means the same as like so lately Jonique and I have been fancying things like mad.

"Here's cocoa!" Jonique said, waving a box. "It's called Dutch and has a kid with a 2-pointed hat."

We made a pact to never wear a hat like that in this lifetime. Then we went to the basement where Madam keeps supplies in case she has to have a big party with no warning whatsoever, which is a thing that happens a lot because she's from Louisiana and that is a state full of celebrators.

"Here's a pack of 100 cups," Jonique said.

"Good," I said. "Cocoa is a popular drink."

February 6

To look good for selling, I wore my sweater that says Knitted in China on its neck and my pink jeans and I tied my bandana around my head for fashion. Then I told Jonique the problem: "Pop drank the milk and all that's left is soy, which I'd say would make ruins of cocoa."

"No doubt," Jonique said. "The bad thing is we'll have to buy real milk with our saved money."

The good thing was Joon at Johnny and Joon's grocery gave us a 10-cent discount. "We small business owners have to help each other," Joon said.

To pay back the favor, we waited until a lady was coming and I said in my loudest voice, "This is 1 SANITARY store and the owners are absolutely LOADED with HYGIENE."

That remark was so pleasing for Joon that her face turned red.

Halfway back it started snowing like a blizzard

so we had to cancel cocoa and watch the movie of
My Fair Lady with Pop who was taking a break
from the emus on account of my mom was at work
and Madam and Mrs. McBee were still at the auction.

P.S. Here's what we can't believe: Milk costs
more than soda.

The same night at 8:50 in the P.M.

When Madam and Mrs. McBee got back they were
feeling too much excitement. "We won some and
we lost some," Mrs. McBee told us. "But at the end
of the day the Baking Divas are the owners of a
walk-in refrigerator, a 40-quart mixer, an ice machine, 6 baker's racks, a huge oven, 27 pans, and a
dozen wrought iron tables with chairs."

"All together it only cost a little more than 1
new walk-in fridge," Madam said. She had the look
that's called triumph and victory.

Then Mrs. McBee said: "We'd better get working because everything arrives in 5 weeks."

Here's what I think: Jonique and I better get

selling because they could go broke with all this cheap buying.

February 7

The 1st thing we did was drag the little table out of the morning room and put it on the sidewalk in front of Madam and Pop's house.

"Is this okay?" Jonique asked me.

"Don't you worry," I said. "Madam told me this table is old and anybody can see it's worn out."

"Then let's cook cocoa," she said.

We poured our milk in Madam's pitcher that's made of green glass. "When the microwave dings, I'll holler for Pop to get it out because that's the rule," I said.

That's when Pop said: "What are you up to?"

"Selling cocoa to make money," I said.

"That's using the old noodle," he said.

To him, noodle is the same as brain.

Then he said, "Madam's in Annapolis giving a speech to the Young Mothers so I'm the only grown-up around and I'm up to my ears in emus. Here are my instructions: Make money. Have fun. Come in when you're cold."

"You make money and have fun writing," Jonique said.

After he left us she asked me, "How much cocoa should I put in?"

"I'd say ½ a can," I told her.

I stirred until the lumps disappeared and Jonique went outside and set up cups and used up Pop's Duck Tape sticking our Cocoa $1 sign to the table.

Then I picked up the pitcher and shouted to Pop, "See you later, my old noodle!"

Old noodle made me think of old poodle so I yelled "Gumbo," and he came skittering on his toenails. I wrapped Pop's scarf around his middle for warmth and we went outside to wait for customers.

"Step right up! Get your red hot cocoa!" I yelled and Mrs. Deutsch did step right up.

After she left, I said, "Maybe our cocoa is too hot."

Jonique was agreeing with that. "I'd say you're right because Mrs. Deutsch made that too-hot face."

To fix it I scooped some snow off the fence and dropped it in the pitcher.

Then we saw Ed Gold balancing himself on sidewalk ice, so I hollered, "I see you're wearing your ear muffins." I always say that joke to him in the winter.

"I NEED hot chocolate," Ed called back.

"Coming right up," Jonique said.

"I had no idea moneymaking is such a snap," I whispered to Jonique after Ed left.

He got to the far corner and turned around to take a look at us. We waved our arms like mad to show customer appreciation. Ed gave us a wave back and put his cup in the trash. He is not one who litters.

"He drank that cup up in a second," Jonique said.

Then we had a business boom. Mrs. Jensen ordered through her car window and our service was so speedy that no cars honked and Mr. Lee loved our cocoa so much he gave us the compliment of saying, "I'm going to take it home to share with my wife."

"We have a flair for raking it in," I said.

"No doubt," Jonique said.

Then we had the worst customer. Ashley clomped up, making snow squish with her real suede boots, and she gave me $5 and said, "I'll buy one."

It was hard to think of what to do because I still felt aggravation with that girl but I remembered that Glamma's sister named Shiralee, who is the owner of the Beauty Spot Hair Emporium, made up a motto and it is: "The customer is always right."

So to act professional, I gave Ashley $4 for change and I said, "Thank you. Please come again."

"Okay," Ashley said.

Then she took a gulp and SPIT IT OUT in a giant spray that made brown dots all over the snow. "This is the most DISGUSTING thing I ever drank," she screamed. "You 2 tricked me!"

"We did NOT trick you!" I said. "It's not disgusting. People have been loving our cocoa all day long."

"That's impossible, Lucy Rose!" she yelled. "It tastes worse than dirt. I want my dollar back."

"NO REFUNDS!" I said in my snappish voice. "YOU are just trying to get cocoa for FREE."

Ashley stomped down Constitution Avenue, pouring a long brown line of cocoa behind her.

Now we have zero customers.

Still February 7, only at 3:19 PM

Jonique and I were carrying the table up the steps at the exact second my grandmother came through the gate with her arms full to their brims of tulips and oranges. Since I had my hands full of table I waved my head at her and called, "Hello, my Madam!"

That excitement made Gumbo jump over the rosemary bush and lick Madam's neck, which gave her the wiggles and right before our eyeballs, her feet got tangled in Gumbo's scarf and her boots slipped on ice, and flowers went flying and oranges went rolling and Madam was skiing straight ahead. I tried to catch her with the table, but Gumbo was going frantic and leaping about so our arms and legs got confused and too much activity made the table slip and then Madam's leg thwacked into the porch railing and it broke. Not the railing, the leg. I mean, not Madam's leg, a table leg.

Pop ran out and saw Madam looking sprawled so he swooped down and picked her up by her armpits. Jonique and I jumped over the lopsided table that had bumped down steps.

"Don't you worry, Madam," I said. "I'll rescue your furry hat from the slush!"

"I never knew tulips were fragile," Jonique said.

"Great news, everybody!" I said. "I found Madam's eyeglasses."

Then I said, "Does anybody know a way to fix toenail scratches?"

Madam didn't and Pop was busy getting her inside and into a sitting situation. Now he's inspecting her bones and I am writing this report.

February 7 at 7 or so at night

The relieving news is that Madam's leg has bruises only. The other news has to do with the table. It is not relieving. Usually, old means old, like Pop is old and Madam is too but now is not the time to say it. It turned out the table is not regular old. It's antique old. It came from Madam's grandmère, who had the name of Mumpsy, and it was old even when Mumpsy was young because it came from France on a boat.

To help Madam feel better, I smoothed her forehead lines with my red knitted mitten and I said, "I'm sorry in the extreme and in my heart."

"Me too," Jonique said. Her face still had the look of being horrified.

"I can fix those legs," Pop said. "All I need is glue for the table and a heating pad for my lovely and flexible wife who flies through the air with the greatest of ease."

Then he made his serious eyes at Madam and said, "I think we can be grateful they weren't selling naps."

"True," Madam said. "I wouldn't want to come home and find our bed on the sidewalk."

"That's using your sunny side!" I said. "We'll get you hot chocolate so you'll feel like you're relaxed and refreshed."

Pop and Jonique heated up the cocoa that was

leftover and I fetched the heating pad from upstairs. Then I very carefully stuffed the tulips into a pitcher that's Madam's favorite because it's shaped like a chicken. Jonique and I put most of those things on a tray with cloth napkins because Madam says they're civilized. She is a fan of civilization.

After we were cozy and Madam's legs were warmed, we clanked our mugs for a toast.

Then we all made lip-scrinching, tongue-sticking-out faces and Pop said, "That's SOME cocoa."

"It needs sugar," Madam said.

"It does?" I said.

"Quik powder doesn't," Jonique said.

"Dutch cocoa does," Madam said.

Even though she was still limpy in her legs, Madam walked to the kitchen and showed us how to make a new batch from scratch with sugar.

"It's D-double-Dutch-D-licious," I said. "But I believe we are going out of the cocoa business."

"At heart it was a good idea," Madam said.

"I'll get another one," I said.

"Of course you will," Pop said.

February 8 at 8:27 AM in the morning

This day started early because I had to have an e-mail chat with my dad. First I told about the cocoa disaster. Then I typed, "Is it snowing in Michigan?"

"No, but it snowed yesterday," he wrote back.

"It's snowing like wild here," I said. "My school is on TV for being canceled."

"I-N-V-U," he e-mailed back.

Most people don't know that teachers adore snow days even more than kids but I do because in the Ann Arbor Junior High teachers' lounge, which I have personally visited, there's a fake snowman that's named Gracious Ruler. He has inches painted on him and when snow gets to his neck, school gets canceled. According to my dad, when the teachers feel worn to pieces and bits by kids, they say, "Oh, Gracious Ruler, deliver us," and even though he's made of wood, they give him cookies.

After breakfast my mom and I did math practice. Now it's time to meet Jonique in front of the

Golds' house and I am glad like anything to let those fractions go.

February 8 *at lunchtime*

What I was not glad about was giving money back. So when Ed opened his door I said, "Ed, I hide."

He made a grin at me and said, "Not very well. I can see you."

"It's a palindrome," I said. "It's also true because I have too much embarrassment over our cocoa."

"Same for me," Jonique said.

Ed said, "I don't mind paying for a new experience and that cocoa was as new an experience as I've had in quite some time."

"We are the kind of sellers who say Satisfaction Guaranteed," I said and gave him back his dollar.

"You keep it," he said. "I'll consider it payment for ed, i hide. I plan on getting a lot of use out of that palindrome."

Jonique was in charge of the next return but Mr. and Mrs. Deutsch were at Glen Echo learning how to dance in a ballroom, which was a miraculous miracle because Mr. Deutsch is one who resists dancing. Jonique gave the dollar to Anna, who is their daughter that's in college, and said, "Please, tell your mom we're sorry about her having that bad taste."

"In her mouth," I said. "Bad taste in her mouth."

"Right," Jonique said. "It's excellent everywhere else."

We put Mr. Lee's dollar in his mailbox.

Mrs. Jensen said, "I should pay you for saving me the calories." But that turned out to be a joke.

Now we're at my house eating egg sandwiches.

We only have 1 person left. "P-U times 2," I said.

February 8 in the afternoon

Jonique and I stewed in the tree box in front of Ashley's house for quite a little while. Then I thought up a happy question, which was, "What if Ashley's visiting her dad and Jennifer, the girl-friend?"

"I wish that would be true," Jonique said.

That idea made us feel like we were a little brave

and we raced up her steps but before we even finished, the door swooped open and Ashley's mom
was saying, "Come on in, girls!"

"We're sort of rushing," I said.

But she was already yelling, "Doll, come down.
Your friends are here to see you."

She calls her Doll because she thinks she is one.

"We want to give her $1," Jonique said.

"How generous!" Ashley's mom said.

"I thought she could be at her dad's," I said.

"Oh, no," her mom said. "He's still in Hawaii."

She sounded a little bit like her teeth were sticking together.

"Without Ashley?" Jonique asked her.

"Of course without Ashley," she said. "Children
don't go on honeymoons."

"Her dad got a new wife?" Jonique blurted.

"He did," her mom said. "They called Doll with
the news from Maui on New Year's Day. They won't
be back until March."

"That's quite the impromptu thing to do," I said.

"You must have picked that word up from
Ashley," her mom said and made a nice look at me.

That's when Ashley came stomping at us, shrieking, "WHAT are YOU 2 doing in MY house?"

"Doll!" her mom said, like she was horrified to absolute shreds.

"Here's your dollar back," I said.

Ashley snatched it and told her mom, "They're NOT my friends. They tried to poison me."

We didn't hear what her mom said about that on account of door slamming by Ashley.

"I can't believe she lied about Hawaii!" I said. "In front of the whole class AND Mrs. Timony."

"Are you going to tell?" Jonique said.

I didn't know the answer to that question.

"Somebody could," I said. "And if I were Ashley I'd fall over in an absolute heap from embarrassment and stay there until I shriveled."

"I couldn't tattle," Jonique said. "Even though she would deserve it."

Then I was quiet because I had thinking to do.

When I was done, I still didn't know what to think about that girl. But to be on the safest side I called my dad and left him a message that said, "DO NOT ever get married without telling me."

That's because it would make me feel like my insides were crushed.

February 9 at 3:22 AM in the morning

I woke up and I had to go in my mom's room to check if she was awake. Then I had to jiggle her head until it turned out she was.

"Ashley's dad got a replacement wife," I said.

My mom sat up fast at that news.

"How's she taking the marriage?" she asked.

"The wife probably likes it," I said.

"I imagine Ashley finds it hard," my mom said.

"Let's be done with the topic of her," I said.

The funny thing is, now I feel like I'm beat tired and exhausted but my mom feels totally awake.

February 10

My dad phoned me and said, "I PROMISE I will NEVER get married without talking it over with you."

"That's the fair thing to do, you know," I said.

"I agree," he said.

"Okay, then," I said.

P.S. The Divas got 2 faucets and a sprayer in the mail. They are not so lovely but they are big.

February 11

After I finish making up so many songs on my cello, I'm decorating Valentines for my entire class, which is the rule but also is a little fake on account of Valentines are supposed to be for TRUE LOVE, which doesn't come over people in 4th. Probably you have to be 19 or 23 years old and most likely you'd have to go to some dances. Also Valentines can be for TRUE LIKE, which is not actually the case for me and every single body in Room 7. But if you skip any person at all you have to go to Mr. Pitt to learn about CONSIDERATION FOR OTHERS, which would be a waste because that's a thing I am already loaded with.

Here are the reasons against making Ashley a card: 1. She lied. 2. She stole impromptu. 3. She is unlikable to me.

Here's what's on the opposite side: 1. I do feel a

speck of sympathy about her dad. 2. I would be peeved if she sold me sugar-free cocoa. 3. Mr. Pitt, of course.

February 12

The UPS lady brought me a box and when I shook it, she said, "Sounds like something good is inside."

She was right because here are the contents of it:

1. Pink socks with red rims.

2. A caramel pecan apple from Kilwin's.

3. A photo of Glam and my dad when my dad was age 9, standing in front of a hamburger stand that is actually shaped like a hamburger.

I put on my socks and stuck the hamburger picture next to my autographed Congressman and I ate ¼ of my apple for a snack. I saved ¾ so I can put ¼ in my lunch and my mom and I can eat ¼ tonight. According to Jonique, ¾ is the same as ½. I'm agreeing with that because, to me, fractions are easier when they're about food.

I made an e-mail that said, "Dear Dad, Thanks a

million. Next time you go to the hamburger place, take me, please. xo."

P.S. Contents is my WOTD. It means things that are inside. Right now my contents are caramel apple and Jonique's Froot Loops plus pomegranate seeds. That's absolutely too many contents because my stomach is so overly full that I'm having to take a little rest.

February 13

I helped Madam staple cloth that's the color of a tangerine on the top of the footstool that she needs to keep her legs in circulation. While I was stretching and she was smoothing the wrinkles, I asked her, "What's your recommendation for people who lie?"

"Is there something you want to tell me?" she said.

"There certainly is not," I said. "I have curiosity and you are an expert, who I'm pretty sure will say, 'Report the lying person to the teacher right away.'"

I did not want to say the person was Ashley because I have an opinion and it's that Madam is too soft about that girl.

"Well," Madam said. "If I had a friend who lied, I think I'd ask myself if the lie hurt anyone. If it did, then I'd tell to protect the innocent person. But if my friend lied to make herself look like a big shot, I'd feel sorry that she felt so unimportant."

"Then you'd tell?" I said.

"I'd talk to my friend privately because I wouldn't want to embarrass her," Madam said.

Here's what I think: Madam was talking about a friend. I am talking about Ashley.

February 14—4:42 PM
Valentine's Day

Valentine's is 1 of my best holidays so I decorated Gumbo, and Pop cooked tomato omelets. We all got heart chocolates except for Gumbo because chocolate is dreadful for dogs. My mom traded me her minty hearts for mine with coconut contents.

Then for a good deed we carried candy to the retired but Mrs. Hennessy took Mrs. Zuckerman's red gumdrops when she wasn't looking. Then she took her purse and Mrs. Zuckerman got peeved at her stealing ways.

Red Alert: Aunt Frankie got 2 Valentines. One from Hank. One from Chester. Hank's has a golden tassel on it.

February 15—School Valentine's Day

Right after the Announcement of the Day that comes from the P.A. system, we decorated Room 7 for our Valentine party and Mrs. Timony said, "Bart and Lucy Rose, I need you to unravel the streamers."

"What's unravel mean?" Bart asked.

"It's the same as pull apart," I said. "I learned unravel when my mom told me to stop doing it to my brown sweater."

The most D-double-D-licious foods were fried

cookies made by Marisol's mom and toffee candy that Hannah got from a store in London called Boots. Now I'm wondering if English people buy their boots at stores called Candy, which I'd say would cause confusion for tourists.

"I brought Red Hots," I said.

"I brought Hawaiian Punch," Jonique said.

"Do they have Hawaiian Punch in Hawaii?" Clayton asked Ashley.

"I don't know," Ashley said.

"But you were there," Clayton said.

"I only drank umbrella drinks," Ashley said.

I looked at Jonique and I could read her mind and we were thinking the same exact thing.

Melonhead's card was a surprise to me, especially after last year, which was surprisingly terrible. This year he drew a giant robot chasing a puny man. Inside he wrote, "FLEE ELF."

"Get it?" he yelled over to me.

"Excellent-O palindrome!" I yelled.

"Thanks for the B-U-T-ful rhyme!" he said.

I knew he would go crazy for it because I wrote:

Violets are blue,
Roses are red,
You're the only one with a Melon
Head.

"My dad says poems are meaningful when they are personal," I said.

Now, here's the rudeness that happened: When the delivery conga line went around, Ashley put an envelope on my desk but inside there was nothing but emptiness. If I were a tattler, she'd be in that old lunch-smelling office of Mr. Pitt's right now.

On the way home Melonhead and Jonique and I sucked Red Hots to turn our tongues red. Hank called us a sight and a ½.

We were, too, especially Melonhead because he wobbled his head and drooled pink spit so it looked like his chin was bleeding to death and caused Mrs. Melon to feel like she could get a heart attack.

For after-school snack Madam fixed parfait that looks like stripes of ice cream only it's made from yogurt and berries and is for my health and I was not in a mood for eating it.

"I'd rather have 67 fire ants in my pants than know that word-stealing, lie-telling Ashley," I said.

"Okay," Pop said. "But it's going to be hard to find fire ants in the winter."

"I'm serious," I said. "She gives me misery and despair."

"What happened?" Madam asked.

"She told every single body in 4th and 5th that I'm in love with Melonhead," I said and I started to cry from the frustration of it. "She's says I gave him a LOVE poem for Valentine's, which I did NOT. Now everybody sings K-I-S-S-I-N-G if I'm near him at all."

"That was a rotten thing to do," Madam said.

Pop gave me a hug and went into the kitchen. I

put my head on Madam's lap so she could call me "Poor Old Sock," and pet my hair for comfort.

"I know you're one who loves looking at people's positive sides," I said. "But Ashley doesn't have one."

"That could be," she said, which was shocking to me.

"Plus she lied about going to Hawaii with her dad, you know," I said.

"I didn't know," Madam said.

After 9 or 11 minutes of hair smoothing, Pop came back with 3 new parfaits.

"The events of the day call for real ice cream," he said.

"Do they ever," I said.

February 17

Even though tomorrow's a school day, Jonique and I got to be the Bingo callers for Game Night at the Home. Mrs. Zuckerman was the 1st winner.

"Please pick a lovely prize from the selection," I said like I was on TV.

"I'll take the striped change purse and send it to my married granddaughter in Kansas City," she said.

"I didn't know married people like change purses," I said.

"Anybody who likes money likes a change purse," she said.

"That includes me then," I said.

Mrs. Hennessy was playing, but not so well. Mostly she was covering up her card with too many buttons.

Mr. Woods was sitting next to a lady with red hair that's new. I mean the hair, not the lady. That gave me curiosity because in my entire life I had never gotten to see a real wig up close, only Halloween wigs and the kind actors wear in plays, which are not so real looking. I got the idea to walk over like I was casual and inspect the lady's head, but only with my eyeballs.

Here's what she said: "Quit hovering."

I had no idea what hover is so Mr. Woods explained that it's when you hang over something.

"Like I'm suspended?" I said.

"Sort of," he said. "But hovering is more annoying."

February 18

At recess Melonhead said, "Wait for me after school."

"I will not," I said. "Ashley could spot us."

"I don't care," he said.

"I do," I said.

"Really?" he asked me.

"Look, Melonhead," I said. "We can do stuff at my house or at the Divas' store but not in front of the public where Ashley can spot us."

Then I walked away.

February 19

When Jonique came to pick me up for school my mom asked her, "Is Adam sick?"

"No," she said.

"Is he running late?" my mom asked.

"He has to walk by himself from now on," I said. "On account of Ashley and the K-I-S-S-I-N-G song."

"Do you really think that's a good solution?" my mom asked me.

"It's a fine one," I said. "I'll still see him, just not where Ashley can see me with him. We're good friends."

I stuffed my feet into my snow boots and grabbed Jonique's arm. Then we scurried right out of my house because I could feel a talk coming on.

February 20

Mrs. McBee is on a campaign to catch up with time so everybody has to scramble like mad, including Mr. McBee's brothers, who drove from North Carolina for 2 weeks of helping Mr. Nathaniel put radiators back where they used to be before the plumbers re-modeled them into vents. They are utterly thankful in the extreme that they got here before the snow did because even though we only got inches and didn't even get off school, they are nervous to drive in it.

The confusing thing about the brothers is they're both named Mr. McBee, but in this book, where I have privacy, I'm calling them Harold and Zeke. They're twins but not the identical kind because Harold is short and a little wideish and Zeke is tall and bounces.

Melonhead thinks the brothers are the greatest because they let him ride with them to the dump, which he says is absolutely full of great stuff.

"Is there stuff people would want?" Jonique asked him.

"Tons," he said.

"That is how we can make Diva money," Jonique said. "We'll rescue treasures and have a yard sale."

"Utterly brilliantine!" I said.

Zeke promised that next time he goes, it will be the girls' turn to ride with him in the pickup truck.

February 21

Here is the e-mail I got from my dad:

"Dear LR,

"You have the TOP SPOT in my heart.

OXOXO,

Daddy"

That palindrome made me feel like I am beloved, which I am. I wrote back:

"Dear Dad,

"My top spot is you. And Mom.

Love,
LR"
I like to be fair.

February 22

Melonhead came over at 8 AM and hollered, "Great news!" through the mail slot and kept saying "Hear all about it!" until I opened. Then he said, "I CAN walk with you in the mornings because Ashley's mom is driving her so she doesn't get cold. She'll never see us."

"Okay," I said. "But if we ever spot her lurking about the sidewalk you have to lie down on the ground and get under snow."

"It's a deal, Lucille!" he said, even though he knows utterly well that is not my name. I am just plain Lucy. Plus Rose, of course.

February 23

Mrs. McBee says if it's not one thing, it's another. Today another is a blocked pipe.

Mr. Jackson the plumber said, "No problem. I'll put a snake in the toilet."

"I would say a snake in the toilet is quite a huge problem," I said.

It turns out the kinds of snakes that work for plumbers are metal, not reptile. Even so, I would not want 1 thing to do with it.

February 24

After cello, Jonique and I went to my grandparents' and found Madam, who was practically done in from too much thinking. She had to come up with a recommendation for a lady called Melting Down in Mount Pleasant who had triplets 5 weeks ago and those babies eat every minute of the day and night and the lady feels like she's absolutely beat and exhausted and, on top of that, her house is a wreck and her clothes don't fit. The 2nd problem was that Madam's editor needed her answer on the double to put it in "Dear Lucy Rose," which is the name of Madam's newspaper column and also the name of herself. So far she'd written: "Dear Melting Down, This is normal."

"Only 244 words to go," Jonique said because that math-loving girl can subtract in her head.

"Here's 3 more," I said. "Buy new clothes."

"Get the husband to clean up," Jonique said.

"I have an idea," Madam said. "While I'm writing, you girls can try on my costume jewelry."

We took that deal but fast. I put 6 bracelets on 2 arms and Jonique put 8 on 1 and we piled on necklaces and covered our hair with bobby pins that have diamonds that could be fake because they came from Grubb's drugstore and I hope they are because we put some on Gumbo, who is not the most reliable poodle. When we were totally gorgeous, I told Jonique, "Madam will feel stunned by us."

I was right about that.

Then I said, "Madam, you should give us this costume jewelry since we wear more costumes than you do."

She did not go for that idea.

February 25

Since I was absolutely weak from starvation and my legs were almost collapsing, Pop took Jonique and me to Jimmy T's for an after-school snack. I said, "Hello, Mrs. T, we seriously need 2 lemon meringue pie pieces, please. With lots of bouncy white on top."

"Bouncy white's the best part," she said.

Pop said, "I'd love a bagel with the Scoop du Jour."

Mrs. T said, "I'll toast your bagel but you'll have to get your own Scoop."

"Don't you worry, Pop," I said. "We've got Scoop galore. Melonhead had to go to Mr. Pitt's office."

"Probably because he climbed onto the roof of the Kindergarten building," Jonique said.

Pop made a confused look at us. "I thought they saved Mr. Pitt for serious problems," he said.

"I think it has to do with Melonhead growing mold in his locker," I said.

"They don't punish people for doing science, do they?" Pop asked us.

"Who knows?" I said. "If I were in charge, I would say falling off the roof was enough of a punishment."

"He fell?" Pop asked us.

"First, he was suspended by his pants," I said. "Then he hovered. Then he fell. But he was a little saved by the holly bush."

"I can only imagine that Mr. Pitt invited Melonhead to his office to congratulate him on his well-developed sense of curiosity," Pop said. "You girls are lucky to have such an interesting friend."

"That's for sure," I said.

"I'm surprised he didn't come to Jimmy T's with you today," Pop said. "He usually will travel for food."

"He couldn't," I said.

To make the subject change, I asked Mrs. T if Jonique and I could refill catsup bottles and luckily she said, "Sure."

February 26

Melonhead's dad brought him to school by special request from the principal, so we had to wait until recess to hear. But 1st I had to make our meeting be in the Kindergarten playground because that's 1 place Ashley never goes. Then Melonhead told us: "When I got to Mr. Pitt's he had his arms folded in that mad way and he said, 'Did you write in the wet cement?' and I said, 'Yes, with a stick.' "

"Seriously?" Jonique said.

"Very," Melonhead said. "You can't make a sharp line with a finger."

"Then what?" Sam asked him.

Melonhead said: "Mr. Pitt said, 'Ah-HAH! I knew it! MANY baseball fans might have written Go Nats! but only 1 would write Melonhead.' So I said, 'Who?' And he pointed at me."

Some 5th graders were piling up around him so he talked louder: "I said, 'I'd NEVER write Melonhead in cement.' "

"Oh, really?" Mr. Pitt said. "Then who did?"

"I don't know," Melonhead said. "But it wasn't me because if I did it, I would write Adam John Melon III, because there's a chance I won't be called Melonhead for my whole life. Then how would people know it was me in that cement?"

Then Sam said, "That's when Bart told me that Melonhead was caught, so I ran to Mr. Pitt's office and said, 'I'm here to take my share of the blame! Melonhead wrote Go Nats! but I'm the one that wrote The Nationals Rule this School!'"

"Mr. Pitt said Sam had COURAGE to tell the TRUTH and that I should have courage and admit that I wrote Melonhead," Melonhead told us. "Since I didn't say it, I have to help Mr. Jackson pick up trash."

"I know you won't do that again," Jonique said.

Melonhead made a shrug. "Wet cement is a thing that's hard to leave alone," he said.

I trust him about that.

MARCH

March 1

Jonique did her report on Virginia because that's where her Granny lives. It turns out that state is famous for making hams. Plus it has so many colleges you wouldn't believe it only I do because Mrs. McBee went to one of them.

March 3

When we got back from making the trash delivery with Zeke, I told Pop, "That dump is a dump."

"You're kidding?" he said.

"I'm not," I said. "There are miles of stuff but who wants a broken hat rack or old hangers or a fan with no blades?"

"Melonhead," Pop said.

"True," I said. "But we need more than 1 customer for a yard sale."

March 4

At recess I told Jonique, "Ashley made Kathleen believe that I'm in love."

"What did you do?" Jonique asked.

"I said I am not and I spent the whole entire morning making pinchy eyes at Ashley," I said.

"Did she shape up?" Jonique said.

"She acted like she didn't even see me," I told her. "So at assembly I said: 'Ashley, 1 thing I am absolutely NOT is in love with Melonhead.' But she said, 'The more you say you're not, the more it proves you are.' "

"She did not!" Jonique said.

"She did," I said. "Then she said, 'Goodbye, Mrs. Melonhead.' Now 3rd graders are copying her."

"She is the worst," Jonique said.

"The worst is that I don't know a way to make her stop," I said.

Actually, I do know a way but thinking about

it makes me feel like I'm not utterly comfortable inside.

March 5

Harold and Zeke are paint blasting, which is exciting because chunks of stuff fly around. Melonhead and Jonique and I had to wear masks and Home Depot eyeglasses because Pop said, "Mr. McBee and I will be in a lot of trouble with the mothers if even 1 of you kids loses an eye."

P.S. The McBee brothers are starting to drive home at 4:30 AM tomorrow morning, on account of they feel edgy if they drive when it's rush hour because Mr. Nathaniel said that's when all the maniacs are out and they don't have common courtesy.

March 6

My mom invited me for a lunch date and since the Greek restaurant is as fancy as the dining room at the Home, I wore my ultra-pink cheetah dress that came by FedEx from Glamma and makes me feel like 1 million. I told my mom, "This dress has so much maturity that Rosemary Joaquin who's in 7th said she wishes it were hers."

"That is remarkably mature," my mom said.

When the waiter came I said, "May I have salad with extra feta cheese but no onions?"

He said, "Of course you may, little lady."

"I told you this is a mature dress," I said to my mom. "He'll probably call you big lady."

"I hope not," she said.

"Ashley doesn't have 1 spot of maturity," I said.

"Is she still calling you Mrs. Melonhead?" my mom asked.

"Yes. Plus she acts like Daddy's poems are bad," I said. "So I say I have a right to tell that she lied about her dad taking her to Hawaii."

"I'd say that's more of a desire," my mom said.

"A desire that I have a lot of," I said. "It's the only way I can make her stop."

"The problem with telling," my mom said, "is that once the words come out of your mouth, you can never get them back."

"I'd say that is the point of telling," I said.

"Think about why she's trying so hard to bug you," my mom said. "Think about why you're letting her decide who can walk to school with you."

"Sometimes I get tired of thinking," I said. "And sometimes I get tired of your thinking, too."

My mom smiled at that and said, "Do you want to split a piece of baklava?"

March 8

For his Georgia report Sam made up a quiz called "Who Calls Atlanta Home?" The right answers were: Martin Luther King, Jr., and the Atlanta Braves and Sam's grandparents and their dog that's named Muffin.

March 9

Jonique wanted me to come with her to the doctor after school but Mrs. McBee said, "Wart removal is not a social occasion."

I would be utterly interested to see how that

doctor gets that wart off her thumb but I am not the sort who begs other people's mothers.

Since I am keeping away from Melonhead I had to walk home completely by myself. It takes longer that way.

March 10

Who knew that paint costs a lot? I did not. But, according to Mr. Nathaniel, the Divas had to spend an absolute fortune on account of their walls drink paint.

That made Jonique and me have an emergency meeting by the 2nd graders' rock garden. When I got home I told Pop, "We are two girls who are completely out of ideas but on the lookout for a fresh moneymaking idea that isn't to do with food or trash and doesn't take eons of time on account of we are short on it because of having to build the bakery and go to school."

"You could always drop out of school," Pop said.

I'm pretty sure that was a joke.

P.S. Wart removal is not as fun as it sounds.

March 12

I told Melonhead, "You HAVE to tell Ashley that you DO NOT LOVE ME at all."

"Then she'll call me Mr. Reilly," Melonhead said.

"I feel like I'm frosted with that lying girl," I said.

March 13

Pop is usually a snoozing man but today he was up and ready to go which was lucky for Melonhead since he was waiting on our steps in 39 degrees.

We took ourselves and 24 sprinkle donuts to work but on the way I had to holler, "Quick! Put your head down!"

"That's a terrible way to drive," Pop said.

"Not you," I said. "Melonhead."

"Why me?" Melonhead asked me.

"We're passing Ashley's house," I said, smooshing his head onto the seat. "She could be looking out the window."

"Lucy Rose!" Pop said in his shocking voice that he hardly ever uses. "We do not hide our friends."

"It's okay," Melonhead said. "I can still eat donuts when I'm folded in ½."

He could, too, because he scarfed up 3 before we parked. To show that I'm a thoughtful friend, I let him put the quarters in the parking meter.

Melonhead spent the morning with Pop prying up bathroom floor tiles. Jonique and I helped Mr. McBee paint outside because that job simply had to be done in case the cold snaps back. Hank and Chester and the Divas went around drawing squares on the walls where they want to plug in electric things.

The peak of today didn't happen until it was almost time to go home and Pop and Mr. McBee and Mr. Nathaniel pulled down the fake wood that was covering the walls in the back room. Peak means the greatest, like Pike's Peak is the greatest mountain, at least to some people. Here's our peak: Underneath the fake wood was a real fireplace.

"This wallpaper can't be salvaged," Pop said.

Salvaged means saved and since it couldn't be we had to get to work pronto. But 1st Pop put boards over the floor holes where toilets used to be before Mr. Jackson took them away. That was so we wouldn't fall in and end up with our legs dangling in the sewer.

Jonique and Melonhead and I got to have the time of our lives spraying the walls with chemicals that I'd say are hardly dangerous and pulling down that ancient paper in the ladies' bathroom. Pop was helping Melonhead scrape the paper in the men's bathroom, which I will not walk in even when there's no toilet. All of a sudden Jonique screamed, "Pop! Come fast!"

He was ultra-speedy in the extreme because he thought we were having a disaster.

"LOOK at the wall!" I said. "Right there! It says Ichabod Turner, June 26, 1869."

"Who is that?" Jonique asked.

"I think Mr. Turner was the man who put up the original wallpaper," Pop said.

"1869 is before they had TV," Melonhead said.

"Or flip-flops," I said. "Or ballpoint pens."

"Or Slip 'N Slides," Jonique said. "Or Cool Whip."

"Or electricity," Hank said because he and Chester heard commotion and came to see.

"Or indoor bathrooms," Pop said.

Melonhead had the look of shock. "I can't stand to think about life before Cool Whip," he said.

Pop fished a Sharpie out of his pocket and pointed. "That small patch of wall is going to be covered by the toilet tank," he said.

We took turns writing our names and our grade and ages plus this date on that wall, so in 111 or more years when they need another new toilet, they'll discover us.

Melonhead wrote one more thing and that was "Cats have 32 muscles in each ear." He figured that the people of the future would like to know that.

March 15

Since school was a ½ day and Jonique had to get her hair fixed by Mrs. McBee, I went by myself to the

Home to help Ms. Bazoo do her social directing. Only there wasn't so much work on account of a lot of the retired were on a shuttle bus trip to Trader Joe's.

"Man alive," I said. "Why would Mrs. Zuckerman go there when the best food on this earth is here at the Home?"

"She wanted to buy dark chocolate because it's good for her heart," Ms. Bazoo said. "And flax oil because she says it's good for wrinkles."

"I'd say she already has enough wrinkles," I said.

Dr. Chu and Mr. Woods are not the shopping kind so they were having a serious chat about the President, who Dr. Chu thinks is doing the job but Mr. Woods says is not the best and he's not keen on his wife, either.

Mrs. Hennessy was sitting on the striped couch having a close-up look at her lanyard key chain.

"How are you?" I said.

"How are you?" she said, and made a huge laugh and patted my fingers.

"Not so great," I said. "Somebody is stepping on my last nerve and her name is Ashley."

"Ashley?" Mrs. Hennessy said.

"Yes," I said. "She's nothing but dreadful to me."

"Dreadful," Mrs. Hennessy said and she made a concerning look.

I told her the whole, bothersome story about Hawaii and Valentines and bad cocoa and the snarkiness. Then I asked her, "Do you think I should tell on her lie, or not?"

"Not," Mrs. Hennessy said.

"Really?" I asked her.

"Really," she said.

"You're a help to me," I said. "And an excellent-O listener."

March 16

Jonique phoned me before school and said, "I'm late. Don't wait."

"That is a circumstance that happens a lot in my house and never in yours," I said.

"Getting this bakery going is making everybody come undone," she said. "Especially me."

March 17 —St. Patrick's Day

Ashley gave me a hard pinch and when I said, "Ouch!" she said, "You're not wearing green."

"My sweater is green," I said. "And my pants."

"Oops," Ashley said. "I didn't see them."

She could be lying about that.

March 18

Aunt Frankie picked us up so we wouldn't have to walk in the rain, which is actually a thing we love to do.

"Guess what?" she said. "I painted the bathrooms."

"Oh, no!" I said.

"Oh, yes," she said. "The color is called Sea Glass. And it will look perfect when we put in the floor tile."

"What's that word for how I feel?" Jonique whispered to me.

"Dejected," I told her.

"That's it exactly," she said.

"What's the matter, monkeys?" Aunt Frankie asked us.

"We didn't want to paint over Ichabod," Jonique said.

It takes all of Aunt Frankie's concentration to park in the city but when she got that job done she said, "Go take a look."

There, in the middle of 1 Sea Glass wall, was a bare square with Ichabod's writing. It is surrounded by a golden frame so now Ichabod looks like he's art. Our names are not framed. They are just waiting to get covered up by a toilet.

"We're done with dejection," Jonique said.

March 19

My dad is one who loves to hear every detail of my life so I told him that the Divas got pantry shelves in the basement and how my mom and I made pizza out of dough. Then we got to Ashley.

"Has she calmed down?" my dad asked.

"Not 1 speck," I said. "She does nothing except call me Mrs. Melonhead."

"I'm sorry to hear it," he said.

"Do you have a way to make her stop?" I asked.

"Have you tried not caring what she says?" he said.

"That's impossible," I said. "It's embarrassing like you can't believe."

"I believe," he said. "She's not an easy girl."

"She is STILL lying about Hawaii," I said.

"That's sad," he said.

"Not so sad," I said. "She is a pain to me."

"She can be both," my dad said.

"You're supposed to be on MY SIDE," I said and it came out testy.

"I'm always on your side, Lucy Rose," he said.

"Good," I said. "Because I figured out a solution."

"I'm proud of you, Lucy Rose," my dad said. "But not surprised. You've always been one smart cookie."

"Thank you," I said.

"Tell me your plan," he said.

"I'll reveal Ashley's lie in front of our class," I said. "So far, the adults are against it but you are a teacher who knows her bothersome ways plus you know how sometimes kids have to learn the hard way, so you can be the one who says, 'Good idea. Go ahead.' "

What he said was, "I know your natural kindness will help you do the right thing."

That was not a comfort to me.

March 20

The Divas and Jr. Divas scrubbed and waxed our arms off and when we were done all I could say was, "Man-O-man alive! This fireplace is a beaut!"

Here's why that's true: It has columns made of oak wood on the sides and the in-between tiles look like Hershey bars with ladies' faces on them. The left lady is staring at the right lady. "I bet they're sisters because they have the same look," I said.

"It's a gorgeous look," Jonique said.

Then Mrs. McBee called out, "Leon, come here."

When he did, she told him, "This back room is going to be a parlor where people can sit and read or rock babies or talk and drink coffee and eat cake."

"Baby, you're a genius," Mr. McBee said.

I would not like it if my husband called me a baby. Genius would be okay.

March 22

I was resting my head sideways under my desk top and reading my dad's poem and Ashley said, "What's so fascinating?"

She was using her snippish voice.

"Something that's private," I said like I was firm.

"A LOVE letter," she said and with no permission at all, she yanked up my desk top and started reading it out loud. Then she stopped and stomped off like she was in a big huff, which is A-OK with me because I am in a huff with her.

Melonhead is in a huff with me because he's tired of walking home by himself. That huff is not A-OK with me.

March 23

While we were at school, Mrs. McBee and Aunt Frankie sanded wood and they had to wear doctor's masks that make their lips sweat but if you don't wear them when you sand, you will end up with painted lungs, which is a perishable thing.

March 24

My Michigan report was excellent-O. My best comment was when Mrs. Timony said, "I like the way you showed us that on the map Michigan looks like a mitten, Lucy Rose. That's something I'll remember."

When I got home I called Shiralee and told her that I made the Spot famous.

March 25

Love Alert: Chester brought Aunt Frankie a box of skinny tube lights for the basement ceiling. "I hope you like them," he said. "They're good energy savers."

Hank gave her bathroom lamps that are completely deluxe because their handles look like hands that are holding up torches. I believe he did it for romance because when Aunt Frankie said, "What do I owe you?" he said, "No charge."

Now Aunt Frankie feels like she's flattered.

March 26

Mrs. Washburn, who is our reading teacher that is quite a bit on the boring side, was doing her adverb talk when Melonhead almost gave me a note but she swooped her arm at him and I don't think she cared about the rudeness of grabbing.

"It's a love note!" Ashley screamed.

That made Bart Bigelow kiss the air 62 or more times.

"It is not," Melonhead said.

Mrs. Washburn tucked the folded paper into her sweater sleeve and said, "Back to adverbs."

At recess, I chased Bart Bigelow until he ran out of air and then I gave him some jabs on his arm and said, "Do NOT make kissing noises about me ever again."

He started kissing the air that instant.

"You were better in 3rd when you picked your nose all the time," I told him.

"I still do," he said.

I do not know why that boy has 1 speck of self-esteem but he has pounds of it.

March 27

Jonique and I went with Mrs. McBee to the Innervision art store to pick up the giant black-boards that Mrs. McBee special ordered so the Divas can have a place to write the bakery contents and prices. That's when we saw Mrs. Mannix and she told us, "I'm getting a papier-mâché kit for Harry because, according to the directions, you have to stay in 1 place to make it. He's too wild and I'm too pregnant to chase after him."

That was as true as could be because at that very minute, Harry was throwing the art store's erasers at his sister named Emma.

"All I want is a place to sit," Mrs. Mannix said.

"I'll have that place in a couple of months," Mrs. McBee said and she told about the Baking Divas.

That news perked Mrs. Mannix right up. "Are you going to sell your Lemon Twist 'n' Shouts?" she asked.

"Of course," Mrs. McBee said. "On cold days you can have them with a cup of tea in front of the fire."

Jonique and I explained our fireplace discovery.

"Really?" Mrs. Mannix said. "When we remodeled, we took down the old mirror with the carved curly-Q wood that was over the fireplace. It's still in my basement. Do you want it?"

Mrs. McBee looked like she was going to faint in a heap on the paintbrush display.

"I would LOVE to have it!" she said.

March 30

We got report cards and I got 1 A and the rest Bs and Cs plus 1 S in gym and a note that says, "Lucy Rose is joyful and creative and a frequent contributor to class discussions," from Mrs. Timony and an added-on note from Mrs. Washburn that says, "Lucy Rose needs to stay seated and stop talking to her neighbors during class."

My mom said I should try to do those last 2 things but Pop said, "At least she's getting exercise and making friends."

Madam just went upstairs and didn't come down for ages but when she did she gave my mom a piece of paper that was her report card from 4th and it said, "Lily, otherwise a delight, is a chatterbox who needs to work on staying in her chair."

I gave my mom a pat and told her, "Don't feel bad. That's just the way it is with us original thinkers."

March 31

After school, Pop and Gumbo and I walked to the Post Office to mail peanut butter to my Aunt Marguerite, who lives in Japan, because it's the American thing she misses most except for me, and I told Pop, "I'm triple tempted to report Ashley."

"You are?" Pop said.

"I am always telling everybody that I'm not in love with Melonhead but, according to Ashley, nobody believes me," I said. "I figured out, if I tell about her Hawaii lie, it will make her turn honest."

"The only person you can make honest is yourself," Pop said.

"I'm honest," I said.

"I'm proud of that," Pop said.

"I cannot believe that I can't get 1 grown-up to agree that I should tell on Ashley," I said.

"Grown-ups can be a disappointing lot," Pop said.

"I am one girl who agrees with that," I said.

APRIL

April 1

Melonhead gave me the greatest thing that Eddie at Grubb's let him have for free because Melonhead is a great experimenter who could use them and also because they weren't selling, if you can believe it. I cannot because who wouldn't want magnet earrings?

The 1st thing I did was show my mom. The next was take a walk around the block so neighbors could admire me but then when I turned on 4th Street there was Ashley coming right at me like I was trapped and all I could think was that it was my lucky break that Melonhead didn't stay after he dropped off the earrings on account of he and Sam were going to take another tour of the FBI.

Ashley got close to me and I made my puniest wave, which is actually more of a hand flop, and she made a handflap back and we almost passed each other and then she stopped and gave my ears such close-up looks that she could probably see my drums and she said, "I see you finally got your ears pierced, Mrs. Melonhead."

"DON'T call me that," I said, but my ears were making me so happy that I had to make my head toss around so she would notice them some more.

"Too bad they're not the dangling kind," she said.

I waited until she got all the way to the corner and then I screamed, "April Fools'! My earrings are made of magnets!"

"You didn't fool me," she hollered back. "I knew it the whole time."

I feel like she did not.

April 3

Madam and Pop took my mom and me on a 3-day surprise trip to Cape May, New Jersey, for Easter. You have to get there by car and by a ferryboat and it is fabulinity.

April 4

First we went to church at Our Lady by the Sea, which was crowded like mad, and then we got samples of fudge from a giant rabbit that was truthfully a person inside a costume. Then we passed a store called Kiss the Cook and Pop kissed Madam and bought her a new spatula that she loves. And then there was a deluxe Easter egg hunt at our grand hotel and we ate ham at the restaurant that's so fancy I was allowed to wear my magnet earrings, which my mom says are not for school or regular life.

April 6

Pop and Mr. McBee are throwing a painting party. They invited my mom and the Divas and Mr. McBee's basketball-playing friends and 2 men from Faith Tabernacle. Since it's Spring Break, Jonique and Madam and I are staying up late and eating spaghetti and fake meatballs that are made out of soybeans but actually taste okay.

My mom and I walked to Art & Soul to buy a present for her friend from college who is having a shower before she has a baby, which I say is a good idea because a person should be fresh when they go to the hospital plus it's good to have hygiene when you're around babies. I think a good present would be soap or maybe a towel but my mom lets me pick the gifts for my friends so it's fair for her to get to pick a pink picture frame for her friend.

All that baby talk made my mom ask about Sam and his sister.

"He's fine," I told her. "Julia the baby can eat cereal made of rice, which I would say tastes like wet paper napkins."

"You loved rice cereal when you were little," my mom said. "You also loved to chew on wet napkins."

"I was gross," I said.

"You were adorable," she said. "Besides, you shunned both once you tasted mashed pears."

"What's shunned?" I asked her.

"It's a good WOTD," she said. "It means you turn away from something. Or someone."

"Ashley is a shunner," I said.

"No," my mom said. "She doesn't avoid or ignore you."

"Well, she is an annoyer," I said. "And a torturer."

April 8

This is the story of last night, according to Madam, who told me, "I woke up at 3:37 with such a grand idea that I had to poke Pop's ribs until he said, 'Ungrugghff.' So I said, 'Do you think Lola could use my extra chandeliers in the bakery?' He said, 'Franggalapppo,' and I said, 'Thank you,' and went back to sleep."

This is the story according to Pop: "I was having a dream about rain and pain and I tried to say, 'Watch it with that umbrella, Buster,' but the jabber kept jabbing until I woke up. Then I thought I heard Madam say, 'Thank you,' but she was asleep."

Now Pop is beat but Madam and the Divas are

feeling dazzled with themselves. Hank and Chester are hanging chandeliers and taking my recommendation about putting the pink swoop one in the parlor where everyone can enjoy a good look at it.

April 9

Pop and I took the Red Line Metro to Salon Familia, which is 1 place that is divine because when you are a girl they give you a free ribbon and I usually pick purple because it looks delightful with red hair.

I had to wait for about 7 or 12 minutes, which was pleasing to me because I got to smell shampoos and look at a magazine about movie stars who are getting a divorce, which was an astonishment to me because who would ever think movie stars would?

When Rosa was done giving a bald man a haircut, which is a waste if you ask me, I said, "Hola."

She came from Argentina, so I say hello in Spanish so she'll feel like she's at home with me.

"You need a haircut, Lucy Rose," she said.

Pop said, "She needs all her hairs cut, Rosa. One hair wouldn't make much of a difference."

He is quite a teaser of those ladies at the Salon.

When we got home I asked my mom, "Did you know movie stars get divorced?"

"I did know," she said. "All kinds of people do."

"If you're a movie star you probably don't care so much because you still get to be in movies," I said.

"I think movie stars care just as much as we did when Daddy and I got divorced," my mom said. "Especially if they have children. Getting divorced is a sad time, whether you're a movie star or a millionaire or a rodeo cowboy or an artist and a teacher and a redheaded girl."

"Is that true?" I asked her.

"It is," my mom said. "Even for a bratty girl with blond braids who has a TV in her room."

April 10

Melonhead telephoned me at 7:13 this morning and said, "Can I come over?"

"You have to walk the long way," I said.

"No I don't," he said. "The coast is clear because Ashley said she'll be at her dad's this weekend."

"Then come on down," I said, like I was an announcer on TV. "You can watch my mom and me give our rug a shampoo."

Melonhead was nothing but jealous of that job and the 1st thing he said when he got to our house was, "Can I have a turn?"

"Be my guest," I said, which showed my thoughtfulness.

"I'm a great guest," Melonhead said.

Then he pushed the foaming soap button 9 times, which is too many.

I didn't say 1 correction about that because I am not the kind who goes around hurting people's feelings.

Plus I was really glad to get a visit with him.

April 11

Disgusting news: Toilets are on the sidewalk in front of the bakery where the public can see.

Jonique and I say that is embarrassing in the extreme but Mrs. McBee says they're a beautiful sight because she thought they'd never get here.

April 12

This is the 1st day back after Spring Break and about 11 minutes after I got to school and before we even had to line up, Ashley saw Melonhead walking a little near me on the playground and she yelled out, "Hello, lovebirds!" and the principal heard.

April 14

Happy Birth Day! That's because Mrs. Mannix had a baby at 4:36 AM and it's named Thomas and is a boy. I say he's bound to be better than Harry, who is a spitter. Thomas weighs 6 pounds and so many ounces, which is more than Glamma's dog named Darling Girl ever will.

April 15

At breakfast Pop said, "Would you and Jonique and Melonhead like to join me at Jimmy T's after school?"

"Jonique and I will," I said.

"Melonhead enjoys a milk shake, right?" Pop said.

"He loves them," I said. "But if he comes there's a chance Ashley could find out."

That conversation of ours made me feel a little sad for a lot of the day. Then at 3 PM I was walking by Melonhead's desk and I surprised myself to pieces because I quietly blurted, "Pop's buying us milk shakes at Jimmy T's."

"Meet you there," Melonhead said, because he knows my rules about walking.

April 16

Mr. Nathaniel said the Divas can't burn wood in the fireplace on account of it's against a code.

"Like Morse?" I said.

"It's city code, kid," Mr. Nathaniel said.

"We don't know that one," Jonique said.

"It's hard to learn and it changes all the time," Mr. Nathaniel said.

"Who needs wood?" Mr. McBee said. "We'll get gas."

"We'll get gas?" Melonhead shouted.

Then he spent the rest of the afternoon making fart noises.

April 17

My mom and I were taking Gumbo for a run in Stanton Park and we saw Mrs. McBee walking home from buying already cooked chickens.

"How's it going?" my mom asked her.

"Slowly," Mrs. McBee said. "Display shelves are so expensive I told Leon, 'We'll have to pick between college for Jonique and cases for cakes.' "

"Really?" I asked her.

"I really said it," she said. "I didn't really mean it. Then I found 2 on eBay. I got them for a steal."

136

Luckily that is only an expression.

"They're 80 years old and made of wood and glass," Mrs. McBee said.

"Madam will be in awe," my mom said.

Awe is like when something is a wonder, which Madam definitely is.

"There is 1 small downside," Mrs. McBee said. "They're in Canton, Ohio."

We had to rush off after that because Gumbo had awe for her chickens.

April 18

Jonique and I got asked to pass salsa during the Fiesta at the Home, so to appear like I was festive I wore my rainbow tights and my plaid swirling skirt that makes me look exactly like I'm a señorita. Jonique looked spectacular too because she had on her heart-covered shirt that was personally decorated by Mrs. McBee. When we got to the lobby the 1st person I saw was Mrs. Zuckerman who was looking deluxe because her shawl came from Mexico ages ago when she was on a cruise with the permanently late Mr. Zuckerman. Dr. Chu tied pom-poms to her walking stand and Mr. Woods had on a sombrero that he got at the Opportunity Shop for a bargain. Mrs. Hennessy was not in a very Mexican mood, unless you count her hair, which was looking a little volcano-ish. According to Melonhead, Mexico is utterly loaded with volcanoes.

"That is SOME hairdo," Jonique said.

"I fixed it with that fixing thing," Mrs. Hennessy said.

"It makes you look taller," I told her.

April 19

Robinson did her South Carolina report and to show a food they love in that state, she gave us boiled peanuts, which were slimy-tasting to me. So for a joke I said, "I am in a different state: the state of despair."

April 20

I told Aunt Frankie the entire story of Ashley. Then I said, "If you had a lying girl like her when you were in 4th, what would you have done?"

"I did have a girl like that," Aunt Frankie said.

"Really?" I said.

"I tried to make her stop," she said.

"Did it work?" I asked her.

"No," she said. "The more attention I paid her, the meaner she got."

"It's the same with Ashley," I said.

"I was practically grown before I figured out why she did it," Aunt Frankie said.

"To make you feel sickening?" I said.

"She did it because she was angry," she said.

"About what?" I asked.

"I have no idea," Aunt Frankie said.

"I could tell our class about Ashley's lie," I said.

The only thing Aunt Frankie said was, "Hmmm."

"Wouldn't you do that?" I said.

"I hope I wouldn't," Aunt Frankie said. "I like to think I'm too big to stoop that low."

April 22

Mr. Nathaniel turned on the walk-in refrigerator in the basement today and he said even though you can open it from the inside, there will NEVER be a circumstance when kids are allowed to walk in it.

April 23

Mrs. McBee got a U-Haul truck but she has to return it because it's rented, not bought. She is going to drive to Ohio and Aunt Frankie is the entertainment because she is going to sing for the whole way there and back, which is 3 days.

Good thing number 1: Jonique is staying at my house because Mr. McBee has to go to his job at the government in the day and work at the bakery at night.

Good thing number 2: Mr. Nathaniel's builder friend has the job of turning a restaurant into a ladies' store so he's taking out 2 of the exact same sinks that the Divas need to put in, and he gave them to us for free.

Luckily, the sinks are not in the state of Ohio, which I know from Hannah's report is called Buckeye.

April 24

This morning, while my mom was painting Baking Divas on the awning, Jonique and I were having a visit with Eddie at Grubb's and a lady came in to buy Berry Merry nail polish because even though she'd rather go to Nail Spa, she said she saves fortunes doing it by herself. Eddie knew that already because he has daughters that are big on professional nails and he could go broke from how many times they go.

"That is a handy thing for us to hear because we are 2 girls that need a fortune," I said and 1 second later, Enchanted Beauty bloomed in my head.

On the way home I told Jonique, "Once we're in the beauty business the Divas will be out of worries."

"How come?" she asked me.

"People pay a lot for beauty," I said. "I know Shiralee's rich because you would be amazed at all the jewelry she orders from TV."

"How much does she charge?" Jonique asked.

"I don't know," I said. "But she gets a lot because plenty of people dye their hair and Madam is one of them and according to Pop that's an expensive hobby."

"Are we going to dye hair?" Jonique said.

"No!" I said. "I was saying that for an example. The only thing we need for Enchanted Beauty is your completely deluxe portable nail kit."

"I have a brand-new 2-sided nail file plus cuticle remover and Tropical Breeze lotion that makes you smell like you're at the beach," she said.

At Jonique's we got Mrs. McBee's mixing bowl and Jonique's kit plus a brush in case a lady needs her hair refreshed.

In my room we found my comb that's hardly ever been used and for decorating we pulled the pink and red striped sheets off my bed. Then we looked outside and I said, "Man-O-man, it's raining like dogs."

"The weather always goes against us when we're going into business," Jonique said.

"That's okay," I said. "We'll start tomorrow. Today we can paint a sign that says: Grand Opening."

I tiptoed into my mom's room and gave her a nose kiss so she would wake up from sleeping in.

"I'm going to Madam and Pop's," I said.

"Okay," she said in her froggy voice. "Do you have plans?"

"We're doing Enchanted Beauty," I said.

"Have fun," she said and in 1 instant she was back to sleep.

Pop only asked us 1 question, which was, "Does this business involve any furniture?"

"Only the outside chairs," I said. "The spa location is in front of the carriage house."

"Perhaps I'll come out in a while and see about getting beautified," Pop said.

"Men don't get their fingernails painted," Jonique said.

"Of course not," Pop said. "That would be nutty. I am talking about my toenails."

He went back to writing about the Chesapeake Bay needing more crabs and we went out to tape up our sign and the hairdo pictures that came from my Beauty Spot calendar. I put 1 of my sheets on the ground for a rug and on top we made an arrangement out of 4 white chairs and a table with a display of our beauty supplies.

Sam's mom was our 1st customer and she said, "Since it's the Grand Opening I'll go wild with Redrazzle."

"You have an exciting attitude," I said.

To speed her along we both polished at the same time. I got a smudge on her thumb so it looked a little bleeding but she said, "No one will notice because they'll be so Redrazzled by my other 9 fingers."

Mrs. Deutsch got clear because it was too hard to decide. Madam only had time to get her hands rubbed with Tropical Breeze. Then Mrs. Timony came, which was the honor of our lives, so I told her, "We're giving you our luxury rainbow polishing."

"Every nail gets a different color," Jonique explained.

"I don't need any special treatment," Mrs. Timony said. "Light pink will be just fine."

"Of course you get special treatment," I said. "You're our teacher!"

After that we had no customers, only Melonhead, so we made him 2 tattoos for free with our Sharpie markers. One is a big red dolphin with 3 babies and the other one is a black snake that goes around and around and takes up his entire other arm and hand.

Then he said, "How much do haircuts cost?"

"We haven't done any haircuts," Jonique said.

"Yet," I said.

"I have $1," he said.

"That's how much they cost," I said.

"Do you know how to cut hair, Lucy Rose?" Jonique asked.

"Don't you worry," I said. "I've seen Shiralee do it tons of times at the Spot."

"Can I help?" she asked me.

"Of course," I said. "We are partners."

I got Madam's kitchen scissors.

"What style do you like?" I asked Melonhead.

"Short," he said and pointed at a calendar picture. "Just don't give me Sweet 'n' Sassy Hair."

"Excellent-O," I said and I started cutting the front so he could see and have confidence.

The thing about bangs is that it's hard to get them straight so then you have to cut the longer side to match the shorter side and then that side is shorter so you have to do the other side again. I stopped when it got to his roots.

Then I told Jonique, "Watch me do this side of his head and then you do the other side."

"Should you be going that close to his skin?" Jonique asked me.

"Don't you worry, Melonhead," I said. "I'll color in the naked spot with a Sharpie."

I watched Jonique do her side and I told her, "You have a gift for haircutting."

Then I evened up my side so it would look like hers because, according to Shiralee, matching the sides is the key to a good haircut.

The back was the easiest, except for the part

where Melonhead's hair is always sticking up on top, which I fixed by cutting it off.

Then I gave Melonhead the mirror.

"Thanks!" he said. "I never looked better."

He gave us his dollar and we gave him a giant glob of kiwi gel for extra customer satisfaction.

"I hope we get a lot more haircuts," Jonique said. "They're easier than nails."

"And faster," I said.

April 26

My mom said I can't come out of my room for any reason WHATSOEVER until I write a letter, which I just finished and here's what it says:

Dear Mrs. Melon,

I am sorry that I gave Adam a haircut without your permission and I am even sorrier that you don't like it and that you were going to get your family's picture taken next Saturday, which is the only time you can on account of Mr. Melon's schedule because he's

always having to travel around with his famous Congressman boss. Plus, I am utterly sorry that seeing that haircut made you feel like you couldn't breathe and, like you told me on the phone, saying, "It will grow back," doesn't really help. But I think it could grow back enough by Saturday that if Adam droops his head so you don't see the spot, maybe you can get those pictures taken anyway.

This money is to pay for that buzz cut that is the only solution.

I am truly sorry in my deepest heart and believe me, I do wish I never did it.

Your friend, I hope,

Lucy Rose

P.S. I think that a long shirt could cover up most of the tattoos and I feel regret galore that another thought I never had was about that marker being permanent. You were right when you said that next time I will. That is for sure.

Pop walked me and my letter to the Melons' house and on the way he said that he usually agrees with my mom about direct approaches and not stewing, but that we could have an exception this time on account of a personal visit from me was not too likely to give Mrs. Melon comfort.

I pushed the letter through their mail slot and rushed back to Pop and we walked as fast as we ever could to Johnny and Joon's Grocery to buy an ice cream sandwich, which we split in ½ and ate while we were sitting outside on the step.

I asked Pop, "Do you feel like I'm terrible?"

"Not at all," Pop said. "I thought it was an interesting haircut. When your mom was your age, she shaved her brother's eyebrows off."

"Did you and Madam get mad?" I asked him.

"No. They weren't our eyebrows," he said. "Uncle Mike thought it was a good look and hair does grow back."

Even though Mrs. Melon told me that saying that doesn't help, it helped me.

"Still," Pop said. "It's probably better to keep haircuts in the family."

"Do you want me to give you one?" I asked him.

"No," he said. "Thanks, anyway."

Now Jonique and I are 100 percent broke.

April 28

When my dad called he asked how Madam and Pop and my mom were and I said, "They are great."

Then he said, "I assume Ashley remains a pill."

"You assume right," I said. "I am tired and sick of her love stories about me but she is unfightable."

"I agree," my dad said.

"You do?" I said.

"If you were my student, I'd say, 'Let it go.' "

"What if I was your student and I said, 'I can't'?" I asked him.

"Then I'd say, 'Student of mine, maybe you can see the truth in what she says,' " my dad told me.

"I feel like hanging up this phone," I said.

"I don't mean that you're in love with Melonhead," he said. "I mean that maybe you can overlook Ashley's remarks if you change the way you hear them."

"Plug my ears?" I asked.

"There are a lot of kinds of love in our lives," he said.

"You are being unclear to me," I said.

"There's the kind of love we have for our family," he said.

"That comes automatically," I said.

"And the love that comes when you appreciate someone," he said.

"I appreciate Johnny and Joon," I said. "And Eddie at Grubb's. And Mrs. Mannix."

"Or when you like someone a lot," he said.

"I have a considerable amount of like loves," I said. "Including Aunt Frankie and Mrs. Timony, and Hannah and a lot of other kids."

"Right," my dad said. "Then there are the people you like so much that you really miss them if they are away."

"Like the McBees, especially Jonique," I said. "And Gumbo, even though he's not a person. And Melonhead. And you more than anyone."

"Exactly," my dad said. "Those are the kind that make you want to do kind things—like how you and Mom and Madam and Pop are helping the McBees and how you visit Mrs. Hennessy."

"Those loves are not the kind Ashley means," I said.

"True," my dad said. "Does it help to think about the other kinds?"

"Not at all," I said.

"I love you," he said.

"Of course," I said. "We have the automatic kind."

April 29

Chester picked up the marble rectangles that Aunt Frankie got from the classifieds so they could turn them into counters so the Divas have a place to roll out their dough. To hold the marble up, Mr. Nathaniel used his own antique legs that he got when a Baltimore library went modern. Now that grayish-looking marble is like a tabletop that goes ½ way down 1 wall and around the corner, with 2 square holes for sinks. Mr. Jackson is putting them in and hooking up those copper pipes the McBees got for free for buying the store. When he's done

I'm going to make a ceremony out of turning on the faucet.

April 30

After school, Jonique and I went to the bakery and sprayed gobs of cleaner on that old marble and dirt bubbled like wild. Now our arms are flopsy from scrubbing but the counters are utterly soft-looking for rock and ultra-white and smooth. I told Jonique, "I feel like we're brilliantine."

"We are," she said.

MAY

May 1

Madam and I had to have a visit with the engraver over a wedding present for her friend's daughter who's marrying late, because she's 46 and has enough toasters.

On the way home we dropped off magazines at the Home. I gave the *Gourmet* with a 4-story cake on its cover to Mrs. Hennessy. She gave me her shoe.

"Thank you," I said because you have to have manners. I put that squishy loafer next to me on the sofa and when we finished admiring cakes, I gave it back.

"I have been looking for that thing," she said.

May 2

When I saw Mrs. Mannix's mirror hanging over the fireplace, I had to make a gasp. Then I said, "It looks more divine than anything a body could dream up."

"The Victorians understood beauty," Mrs. McBee said. "Look at the side shelves and the carved flowers."

According to Mrs. McBee those Victorians lived ages ago and they loved everything to be fancy with details. According to Mrs. Mannix they loved everything that was fussy and overdone.

"Jonique and I are fans of overdone," I said.

May 3

Ashley said she could not do her report today because her head was aching from hay fever.

If I were Mrs. Timony I'd tell Ashley, "I have had it with your excuses."

The giant oven gets hooked up tomorrow by Mr. Jackson, who's also in charge of the exhausting vent that lets smoke out of the store, plus he's putting in the fire extinguishers that cost a boatload.

Jonique and I went to Johnny and Joon's to buy orange Mentos because Pop said we could for a treat and Johnny said to me, "I hear you have a boyfriend."

"I do not," I said.

"He's a nice boy," Joon said. "Last time he was here he put banana stickers all over himself."

"If I ever do have a boyfriend I won't have the kind that wears fruit stickers," I said.

Then I felt bad because it's actually hilarious in the extreme when Melonhead does that, especially when the stickers are hanging out of his nostrils.

"Did Ashley tell you he's my boyfriend?" I asked.

"No," Joon said. "I heard from Teddy Joaquin."

"Oh, brother," I said. "If a 2nd grader knows that lie of Ashley's, everybody on the Hill has heard it."

P.S. Madam and Pop are in St. Michaels, Maryland, having a romantic getaway, which is not a thing I like to discuss.

May 7

The good thing about that getaway is Madam and Pop brought me a cheesecake that is so puny I could eat it in one bite, only I didn't because I shared it with Jonique. It came from their hotel that's called an Inn.

May 8

Mr. McBee and Jonique got Mrs. McBee a Mother's Day present of professional knives and bowls and spoons and cake stands and huge measuring cups plus 2,000 white bags for customers and on the bow Jonique tied a thing made of wire ovals that's for whipping. It's called a whisk.

May 9–Mother's Day

My mom scrambled eggs with her new whisk that she loves and I made myself out of wire from our basement.

She's also wild for my card that says, "WOW MOM."

"It's an upside-down palindrome," I said.

My mom turned it and said, "Wow, Lucy Rose. That's amazing."

"Daddy taught me that trick," I said.

I didn't want to steal his credit.

May 10

I would say Mrs. Mannix has told every Mom on the Hill about Baking Divas, which is good for business and for the parlor because a M.O.T.H. who heard gave the Divas a chair and a green sofa from the Victorians because she's moving to Seattle, Washington, without them.

According to Clay's report that state is rich in rain and apples.

May 11

Jonique and I went to check on the Divas and got stunned to pieces because the wall that was white is painted with sky and clouds and giant Divas wearing chef hats and smiling their lips off. All around them are flying cupcakes and floating pies and strawberry shortcakes and birds with sparkling heart cookies in their beaks.

High on the ladder, almost to the ceiling, was my mom with a paintbrush in her hand and another 1 in her teeth and blue paint on her chin.

"It's D-double-D-vine!" I told her. "I feel proud of you."

May 12

Mrs. Hennessy has gone wild for barrettes so Jonique brought her 2 that have yellow twirls and clipped them in her hair, which I think she loved because when she saw herself she said, "I'm swink!"

"That's a WOTD," I said. "What does it mean?"

"No one knows," Mr. Woods said.

Then he said, "Mrs. Hennessy loves your visits."

"She doesn't remember our names," Jonique said.

"She usually calls me Friend," he said.

"Sometimes Spicy Friend," I reminded him.

"Spicy suits me," he said.

Then he told us about Mrs. Hennessy and when he got done, I ran out so fast that Jonique couldn't keep up but I couldn't slow down. When my mom came to pick me up at Madam and Pop's, she found me in my room rolled up in a ball of quilts, crying my head off.

She kneeled down next to my bed and said, "What's the matter, honeybunch?"

"Mrs. Hennessy has old-timer's disease and she's going to forget me. And Jonique and everybody, even her son," I said.

"Oh, that's very hard," my mom said.

"She already doesn't remember how to tie shoes," I said. "Or put on barrettes or flatten her hair. She forgets easy words and gets stuff wrong and does odd things like giving me her shoe and it's going to get worse."

"I'm so glad she's in a nice place where kind people can help her," my mom said.

"I don't ever want you or Daddy or Madam or Pop or Glamma or anybody to get old-timer's," I said and that idea made me feel weepier.

"Most people don't get it," my mom said. "And the people who do get it tend to be old. Daddy and I and even your grandparents are much younger than Mrs. Hennessy and by the time we are her age, I think scientists will have figured out a lot more about Alzheimer's disease."

"I wish she'd get better," I said.

"I wish that too," my mom said.

"Is it going to make her late?" I asked her.

"What do you mean?" my mom said.

"The permanent kind of late," I said and I could not stop crying from the sadness of that.

"Some people with Alzheimer's live for years," my mom said. "But some don't."

May 13

I was 2nd in line this morning and I was standing
quietly and thinking about how to be a good friend
of somebody who forgets who you are and that's
when the dreaded Ashley said, "Excuuuse me, Mrs.
Melonhead," and butted in front of me.

I was trying to dream up a snappy comment and
all of a sudden I knew the exact thing to say and it
was not 1 speck snappy. It was, "I am ashamed to
know myself."

Ashley said, "Because you are a LOSER."

"No," I said. "I'm ashamed that I've been shunning
Melonhead because I don't want people to believe you
about me being in love. But in that instant that was 1
instant ago, I figured out that I DO NOT CARE what
you tell people because he's my great friend."

"That's the same as in love, Mrs. Melonhead!"
Ashley said and made a twisty face that was mean
as could be and lots of things came rushing into my
mind and one was what my dad said and another
one was the melting witch from *The Wizard of Oz*.

I looked right at her eyeballs and said, "I am utterly over you, Ashley."

Ashley's face was hanging from shock. My stomach was overturning, which it deserved because now that I had sense about it, I was feeling like I was horrified with myself.

I ran to the far side of the playground, which is where Melonhead always stays until the last split of a second before the bell rings. He was whooshing down the slide, headfirst, so I stood at the bottom and when he landed I said, "I never did anything this terrible in my life and I am utterly sorry."

My eyes were full to their brims with crying so I had to wipe my sleeve over them.

"Allergies," Melonhead said, to save me.

My nose snurfled. "My state is misery," I said. "You are my brilliantine friend who is my 2nd best after Jonique plus you gave me your magnet earrings and you trusted me to cut your hair and I was being a crummy friend with no thoughtfulness whatsoever and making you feel like you were shunned to pieces."

"You were quite crummy," he said. "I'm glad you are coming back to yourself."

"I am back," I said. "Completely because I have learned this lesson."

Then I had to ask him, "Did I hurt your feelings?"

"Yeah," he said. "But don't tell anybody."

"Can we be salvaged?" I asked him.

"Sure," he said. "I get over things."

Then I had the feeling of a little panic.

"I don't mean the kissable kind of friend," I said.

"If you did, I'd be running so fast your head would spin," Melonhead said.

That remark gave me the snorting kind of laugh.

May 14

My dad and I played Boggle over the phone. It was easy because we each have our own game. I won most of the times.

May 15

This was an all-paint day. My job was a baseboard and Jonique did 2 windowsills and Pop and Melonhead did the front door. The Divas and my mom and Mr. McBee and Mr. Nathaniel did the biggest job, which was the walls in the parlor.

That job took practically the whole day long. When everything was done, Mr. Nathaniel made an inspection. Then he gave Melonhead a look and said, "Boy, run up the ladder and paint that spot I missed near the ceiling."

"Yes, sir!" Melonhead said and if you saw his happiness you'd think he won 1st prize.

"Take 1 rung at a time," Mr. Nathaniel said.

That comment was a good one because Melonhead is the sort of boy who skips.

The other reward for everybody was to eat dinner at the Thai restaurant. Their food comes from Thailand and is delicious plus a lot of it is fried. Only Mr. Nathaniel couldn't come because he was waiting for the gas man who promised to be there at 3 PM in the afternoon but wasn't.

May 16

Mrs. McBee e-mailed us a message that said: "Come into my parlor."

When we got there she flipped the light switch and I said, "Oh, my stars!"

"Mercy!" Jonique said.

"Magnificent!" Madam said.

Instead of turning on chandeliers, that switch turns on a fire in the fireplace and you can hardly tell that the logs are fake because the fire is actual.

"You are going to have customers galore," I said.

May 17

I was supposed to be doing my homework when my brain started storming with my most brilliantine idea and I had to quit reading about Utah and collect all our magazines. Then I cut out a cartoon man and a real watch from the *New Yorker* and a duck and a shoe and a bed and a lady and a ball from my utterly ancient coloring book. I cut up the Zingerman's catalog so I had a sandwich and cake and candy and cheese and bread. When I had a stack I glued every picture on its own page. Then I stapled a lonely sock to another page and taped one of my mom's keys to its own paper. I drew pictures of a hat and a lamp and a fork and eyeglasses and a pen and a daisy and pasted a fake dollar bill that came from Pierra Kempner's birthday goody bag. Then I peeled labels off our cans and glued down peas and carrots and corn and beans and yams and beets. Plus, I found a picture of a panda in *KidsPost* and a sofa and dress in the regular *Post*. And the last thing I got was my school picture of me wearing my vest that my Great Aunt Ginny made out of patches with my yellow bandana tied around my head. I didn't stop pasting until I made 146 pages.

Madam let me use her 3-hole puncher, which is not the easiest thing, and she gave me the kind of blue notebook that people get in high school and she gets to keep her newspaper columns in. On the front I wrote, "Things to Remember."

When I showed my mom she said, "You are a true friend."

Then she said, "I guess we'll be having surprise dinners for a while."

That's because we don't know what's in those naked cans.

May 18

I gave Mrs. Hennessy "Things to Remember" and I explained, "It's to help get your words back."

We looked at page 1 and I said, "cat," and she said, "cat," after me. We kept on until page 27, which was enough for 1 day.

Then I said, "Goodbye," and she said, "Goodbye, bird!" and when I left she was hugging her book.

That made me feel like I had goodness inside.

May 19

Today was fun but not the most successful because Mrs. Hennessy forgot all the Words to Remember.

"We'll just keep doing it until they stick," I said and we started up again with cat.

Later, when Jonique and I were leaving, Mr. Woods asked us, "How did it go today?"

"I figured out the words probably won't stay for long," I said. "But she has interest in looking at the book and saying the words. It's like an activity."

"She likes the baby and the apple pictures best," Jonique said.

"You've been good friends to her," Mr. Woods said.

"She's a good friend too," I said.

"Would you girls care for a Life Saver?" he said.

"Would we ever," Jonique said.

He took a ½ roll out of his sweater pocket and peeled 2 off and gave Jonique a red one and I got green, which I put right in my mouth.

"Mmm," I said. "Linty but refreshing."

May 20

I almost collapsed out of my desk chair when Mrs. Timony said, "Now, representing the great state of Hawaii, I present: Ashley!"

I clapped because that's just polite.

Then Ashley said, "Instead I'm representing the great state of Maryland."

Mrs. Timony looked like she was feeling surprise galore over that but Ashley kept telling the class, "Maryland is an interesting state because it has crab cakes, the Orioles, the Baltimore Aquarium and White Flint Mall and farms and a beach that leads to the Atlantic Ocean."

She talked her head off for minutes and she showed a picture of the state flower, which is called Black-eyed Susan and a post card of a restaurant in Annapolis. Then she said, "Does anyone have a question?"

I raised my hand but she skipped me until there was no one else left and Mrs. Timony had to make the recommendation of calling on me.

"How come you didn't do your report on Hawaii, Ashley?" I asked and I looked at her right in the eyeballs.

She looked right back in my eyeballs and gave me a stare and the thing I noticed was that her hands were shaking and she was looking altogether twitchy. That made me remember the impromptu concert and my queasiness and sweating from nerves and embarrassment and how everybody was watching me and Jonique and how Ms. Bazoo saved us.

"I picked Maryland since I was born there so it's the most important. To me, I mean," Ashley said, and her eyeballs got squinty like she was scared somebody was going to throw something at her.

"That's a good reason," I said.

May 21–8:11 AM in the morning

When the doorknocker knocked my mom was ironing her skirt for work so she said, "Can you get it, Lucy Rose? That Adam comes earlier and earlier."

I multi-tasked like mad and slid down the banister while I was brushing my teeth and when I opened the door I had Crest foam on my lips.

It was Ashley.

Here's what she said: "Hi, Lucy Rose."

That's when I remembered the Melons went to Florida for 3 days.

"Hi," I said.

"You knew I didn't go to Hawaii with my dad," Ashley said.

"I didn't know that you knew that I knew," I said.

"I just found out last night when my mom told me that she told you about my dad getting married a long time ago," Ashley said.

"In January," I said.

"How come you didn't tell everyone I didn't go to Hawaii?" she asked me.

"I really wanted to tell," I said.

"Why didn't you?" she asked.

I did not want to say about every grown-up telling me not to do it, or that I'm glad in the extreme that my dad didn't go to Hawaii and marry some girlfriend. And I didn't think I should say that when Ashley was in front of our class looking scared and lonely and unbeloved, I felt sorry for her.

What I said was, "Probably it was because of my maturity."

Then I thought what if I sound like I'm showing off so I thought fast and remembered how Madam says most things have some good in them, and I said, "If the circumstance was opposite and I was the one who told the lie, you would do the same thing I did."

"No, I wouldn't," Ashley said. "I would have told."

That made my face feel like it was red and steaming and my hands turn into fists on my hips. "Why on earth would you want me to feel like I was embarrassed to shreds?" I said.

Ashley just rolled her eyes at that and started clomping down the steps. When she got to our flowerbed that's made of yellow pansies, she turned around and said, "You have everything, Lucy Rose." It was in her ultra-snarkiest voice.

I did not get that at all.

So I called out, "I don't have a TV in my room."

I went back inside and started telling my mom the whole shocking story and all of a sudden, I had one of the biggest thoughts of my life and I turned around and ran after that girl.

When I finally caught up, which was not until East Capitol Street, I hardly had a breath left in me. I asked her my question.

"The answer is yes," she said. "But if you tell, I'll say you're lying."

May 22

I got a package from Next Day Mail and inside was a book called *Tom Swift* that used to be my dad's when he was in 4th and inside were 4 cards and they were all aces and a note from my dad was with them and it said: "You're aces in my book." That is the same as being great.

May 23

The Divas are rich in flour. Also sugar. The shelves are full of cinnamon, and baking powder and vanilla and lemon extracts, and Dutch cocoa. To help out I wrote NEEDS SUGAR on that box. The walk-in fridge is jammed with 50 pounds of butter and piles of chocolate chips and umpteen gallons of cream and 290 eggs. When the Divas looked at it, Mrs. McBee said, "Let the baking begin."

It's for practice to see how the oven works.

May 23-6:03 PM at night

When Melonhead got back from Florida, Jonique and I raced over and Mrs. Melon answered and I was nervous because what if she still remembered the haircutting incident?

Luckily, Melonhead answered the door. Mrs. Melon was watching the news with Mr. Melon and they were not paying 1 dot of attention to Melonhead because that Congressman boss might be telling his opinions on TV.

I hollered out, "Ashley did it!"

"Did what?" Melonhead said.

"Wrote Melonhead in the cement," I said. "First thing in the morning, I'm going to tell Mr. Pitt on her so you'll be out of trouble."

"Don't!" Melonhead said. "Please, Lucy Rose."

"What on earth?" I asked him.

"I LOVE having my name in cement," he said. "Now I'm famous in the 5th grade. Melonhead will last forever, like Ichabod. I have the glory!"

"But you had to do her punishment," Jonique said.

"I know," he said. "Mr. Johnson let me squeeze his mop in the automatic wringer. I had the time of my life."

May 24

At 4 PM in the afternoon, the Divas and Madam took a latte break and Jonique and I took it with them only Madam got us All Natural Boysenberry juice. Mrs. McBee and Aunt Frankie had to have double espressos on account of they were about to fall over from being exhausted.

"My get-up-and-go got up and went," Aunt Frankie said. Then she laughed her head off.

"I've got bags under my eyes," Mrs. McBee said.

"You most certainly do not," I said. "I don't even know why you would say such an impossible thing."

"Thank you, Lucy Rose," she said.

"The only thing you have under your eyes are those dark smudges from not getting your sleep."

Aunt Frankie laughed so hard her coffee sloshed.

"You are one jolly lady," I said and Jonique agreed about that.

May 25

Mrs. Zuckerman telephoned the Divas and invited them to the Home for a visit. Since they are not ladies who like to say no to the retired, they had to get cheerful fast, which is not the easiest when people are feeling utterly overwhelmed, which they were completely.

When we got there, a lot of the retired were in the lobby and Mrs. Zuckerman and Mr. Woods were sitting by a tray of flowers. "These Sweet Williams are for the store front," she said. "Emanuel and I grew them from seeds."

"Why, thank you," Mrs. McBee said.

"Flowers give customers a good 1st impression," Mr. Woods said.

"Yes, sir. They do," Aunt Frankie told him.

Now those Williams are planted in window boxes. That is thanks to Melonhead and Sam.

At morning greetings Mrs. Timony said, "Does anyone have anything they want to share?"

Jonique told about the Grand Opening that's in 4 days and when she was done, everybody clapped and Bart Bigelow said, "Jonique, since we're in your class do we get stuff for free?"

"No," I told him. "It certainly does not."

Madam cooked all the livelong day and everybody came over to help themselves to chicken and corn on the cob and salad.

But before we ate, Mr. McBee clinked a spoon on his iced tea and when everybody paid attention Mrs. McBee said, "I have always known you all were good people and good friends. But I didn't think it was possible for anyone to be this good. Lucy Rose, I thank you for your original thinking that led you to come up with the Save the Day Plan."

"Now I call it my Salvage the Day Plan," I said.

Mrs. McBee smiled and said, "I'll be forever grateful to you and Jonique and Adam. I never saw children work as hard as you 3 did."

Then she said, "Madam, Pop, and Lily, I hope that 1 day I am given the chance to help someone else as much as you've helped us. I don't know how we would have done it without your faith and hard work, the swooping chandeliers, the incredible mural, the pep talks and great ideas, and your taking good care of my precious lamb while I worked on the store."

Jonique is the precious lamb.

Aunt Frankie said, "Mr. Nathaniel, Hank, Chester and the McBee men, thank you for your expert help. The City Inspector said he had never watched over a building where everything passed the 1st time."

"This is truly a community bakery," Mr. McBee said.

Then we had to eat in a rush because the Divas and Mr. McBee and Pop and Hank and Chester and Harold and Zeke, who came back yesterday, and Mr. Nathaniel had to go back to the store to fix up a few more things before the Grand Opening.

May 28—9:37 still at night

Jonique and I are in my room, lying under my red and pink sheets that have little dots of Redrazzle fingernail polish on the fold-down part and eating raisins. We can't get to sleep on account of having too much enthusiasm over the Grand Opening.

"I'm so happy my mom got an employee so she'll be at home more," Jonique said.

"Ditto," I said.

"But I feel sorry that our moneymaking plans were flops," Jonique said.

"We made money," I said. "We just had to keep giving it back to the original owners and Mrs. Melon."

"We truly were a help with the fixing up," Jonique said.

"Huge helps," I said. "I feel proud of us."

"Me too," Jonique said.

I am stopping this report this second because I hear my mom's legs coming up the stairs.

May 29—Grand Opening Day
6:02 AM in the morning

My eyes are popping out of their lids from the thrill of today. I am up and dressed in my blue plaid shorts and orange shirt and my magnet earrings because this is the greatest occasion. Even my hands are looking festive because of having purple and green ink on them from yesterday when we were helping stamp Baking Divas on 536 white bags and 207 white boxes.

Now I'm standing on my bed, writing in this book, singing, "I'm a Ding Dong Daddy from Dumas" and making dents in the mattress with my boots in case it might wake up Jonique and it just did.

The Grand Night of Grand Opening Day

When we got to 7th Street we felt stuffed with joy. That's because the street was utterly clogged with so many people and the only reason they were holding their horses at all was that Melonhead and Sam were giving samples.

"They LOVE the Fudgalicious," Sam said.

"They LOVE the Glory Bars," Melonhead said.

"They LOVE everything," Sam said.

"Lucky we know how to get in the back way," I said.

When we did get in I could not believe the beauty of that store. It had the divine smells of cooked butter and squeezed oranges and cinnamon and chocolate and coffee. My mom's mural was dazzling the customers. The racks were full of cooling muffins and the white marble counters had cakes and pies and baskets that were full to their brims of brownies and blondies and cheese straws. On the back counter all the boxes we folded were stacked up taller than Mr. McBee and the employee, who has the name of Jean, was filling up a cellophane bag with Aunt Frankie's Famous Sesame-Cranberry-Coconut-Almond Granola and all the workers were wearing aprons that say "Real Vanilla! Real Butter! Real Good!" They were made by my mom. The glass fronts of the display cases were clean like a whistle so customers could get a view of everything on the inside. When I looked at that store, it made me feel like we were great.

"Hello, friends!" Mrs. McBee called to us but she couldn't stop because she was selling at top speed.

"You look completely beautiful, my Divas!" I said. "Your eyes are full of glitter!"

"That's because we haven't been to bed," Aunt Frankie said and put 12 Snickerdoodles in a bag for a man who was not the most patient.

Mr. McBee packed a box for a lady with a

newish-looking baby strapped on the front of her, who said, "We'll have 1 Big Dream Bar and a piece of Humble Pie."

That's when a girl teenager told Aunt Frankie, "I'd like 6 Lucy Roses, please."

"There is only 1 Lucy Rose," I said.

Mrs. McBee took out 6 little cupcakes that had green leaves and sparkling apricot roses on the tops and then she told the girl, "You know, Lucy Roses are twice as good when served with Sweet Joniques."

Jonique started jumping and pointing at the blackboard on the wall. "We're cookies!" she said.

"Our names are on the board!" I said.

"We cost a lot!" she said.

"Finally, we're making money for the Divas, if you can believe it!" I said.

"I do believe it," Mrs. McBee said.

"Me too," Aunt Frankie told us.

One other thing: We are utterly delicious.

Shhhh!

Secret recipes from the Baking Divas!

Lucy Roses

Makes 12 regular-size cupcakes

3 cups of grated carrots
1 cup of canola oil
1 teaspoon of vanilla extract
2 cups of sugar
4 eggs
2 cups of all-purpose flour
2 teaspoons of baking soda
A good pinch of kosher salt
1½ teaspoons of ground-up cinnamon
38 or so raisins

According to Madam, these cupcakes are loaded with health because of having carrots and raisins and canola oil. You can pack in even more health if you add two handfuls of chopped-up walnuts but I don't on account of I already have health galore.

First have a grown-up help you preheat the oven to 350 degrees and put paper muffin cups in a cupcake pan. They will fit exactly.

Next put all the carrots and the oil and vanilla and sugar in a giant bowl. Then crack the eggs on the side and dump the egg contents on top. Then turn on the mixer and mix your heart out.

When it looks very smoothy, turn off the mixer and add the flour and the baking soda plus the salt and cinnamon and raisins and blend it all together. Also, throw in those walnuts if you're going to have them.

When that is finished, use a little measuring cup to scoop out batter and pour it in the muffin cups but don't fill them up to the very top or it will cause burning. Cook the cakes for 20 minutes and then have a grown-up help you do a test by poking a toothpick in one of them. If it's done it will come out looking like it's new but if the cake is still raw the toothpick will come out with hot batter on it and you'll have to cook it for 3 more minutes and then test it again.

Now for the frosting:

1 stick of real unsalted butter

One 8-ounce rectangle of cream cheese and not the diet kind either

2 teaspoons of vanilla

1 teaspoon of concentrated frozen orange juice straight out of the can

1½ cups of confectioners' sugar

Now, put the butter and the cream cheese in a bowl and turn the mixer on medium and mix away. When they are all the way blended, add the vanilla and frozen orange juice concentrate and mix them in. Add the sugar one scoop at a time but turn the mixer off before you pour. Otherwise that sugar blows everywhere, which is a thing that gets on my mom's last nerve.

When the cupcakes are completely cool, put a pretty big blob of frosting in a teacup and a not so big blob in another teacup. Then spread the rest of the frosting all over the cupcake tops. When that is done, get the teacup with the big blob and mix in the puniest drop of orange food dye—or even punier drops of red and yellow—and stir until that icing looks glorious and orange. Then put a puny drop of green food coloring in the other teacup and stir it around. Then put the green icing in a pastry squirter and squirt out some leaves. They don't have to look perfect because a lot of real leaves don't either. When that job is done, fill up a clean pastry squirter bag with the orange icing. The trick here is to squirt it out at the same time you are making your hand go in a circle. When Mrs. McBee does this, they come out looking like real roses. My roses are what's called abstract. But they are still delicious.

# Sweet Joniques

Part 1

2 sticks of unsalted butter
1 cup of brown sugar
2 eggs
1 tablespoon of vanilla extract
2 cups of all-purpose flour
1 pinch of kosher salt
¾ teaspoon of baking soda
2 cups of chocolate chips

Part 2

2 more cups of chocolate chips
One 8-ounce can of sweetened condensed milk
2 teaspoons of vanilla extract

Part 3, which is optional. That means extra so you don't absolutely have to do it.

1 cup of chocolate chips
1 cup of cocktail peanuts (the salted kind)

Have a grown-up help you preheat your oven to 350 degrees.

Put the butter and sugar in the bowl and mix them up with a mixer until those two things are completely blended together. Next, put in the eggs and the vanilla. Also put some vanilla behind your ears because it makes an excellent-O perfume. Then turn the mixer back on and mix until that's done and turn it off. Now add in the flour and salt and baking soda and chocolate chips and mix away until it looks exactly like chocolate chip cookie dough.

> **Here is advice:** Do not mix for too little time because getting a lump of baking soda in your mouth is a disgusting thing. Also do not mix for too long because it will make the dough feel like it's tough.

When all of that is done, rub the slippery sides of the butter wrappers all over the bottom and sides of a 9x13-inch pan. Then take half of the cookie dough and use your fingers to press it in the pan so it is very even.

Now for Part 2: Put the chocolate chips in a bowl and microwave them for 90 seconds and get a grown-up to take them out for you. They will look pretty much like they are still regular chocolate chips but when you stir them they'll turn into melted chocolate. When that chocolate is completely smooth, pour in the can of condensed milk and stir until no white streaks are left. Then stir in that vanilla and let the whole thing cool down until the mixture is looking a little thick. Next spread it all over the top of the cookie dough.

When that is done, make balls that are as big as a walnut out of the rest of the cookie dough and put them all over the top of the chocolate and have your grown-up friend help you put that pan in the oven and cook for about 20 or 25 minutes until the top looks golden brown and divine.

If you want to do Part 3, which I always do, wait until the Sweet Joniques come out of the oven. Then drop 1 more cup of chocolate chips all over the top and after 5 or so minutes those chips will be melty and you can swirl that chocolate all over the top. Then, right away, drop on the peanuts.

Go outside and scooter or something and by the time you come in they'll probably be cool enough for a grown-up to cut up. Then you'll have 32 Sweet Joniques and the thing that is for sure is you will utterly love them.

About the Author

Katy Kelly has never worked in a bakery but she is very fond of cupcakes, particularly the kind that are loaded with icing. (Luckily her daughters, Emily and Marguerite, make them exactly that way.) Katy lives and eats cupcakes with her husband and those baking daughters in Washington, D.C. But most of the time she's busy like you can't believe, thinking up big adventures for Lucy Rose. *Lucy Rose: Working Myself to Pieces and Bits* is her fourth book for young readers.